Where The Rainbow Ends.

By

Sue Lacey was born in 1948 in Kent. Youngest of three sisters, she was always lacking in self-confidence, spending much of her time alone with her head in a book. Books became her friends and, along with her love of animals and in particular, dogs and horses, she would lock herself away in her own little world.

When the family moved to Cornwall she was just a few weeks from taking GCE exams, but felt out of place in the new school, and so, at fifteen, chose to leave and take up the offer of a job on a farm. Being amongst ponies, lambs, cows etc., she was in her element, and back then exams didn't seem as important as they do now.

Six years later she moved to Cambridgeshire, where she eventually married in 1973, becoming a family with one son in 1975. Any idea of further education had not occurred to her until she watched with pride as her son received his degree. Beginning a journey through evening classes to achieve both GCSE and A Level English at a local school. She then ventured on, with limited expectations, to attempt an English and History Degree, finally following in her son's footsteps by being awarded this.

By this time Sue was sixty years old, but it took nearly another ten years before she realised that perhaps it was time to put it to use. She has now done just that by publishing five novels, this one being third in her Steve Lockett trilogy, following on from 'Where Am I?' and 'Where There's a Will'.

<u>Books by Sue Lacey include:</u>
'What Lies Behind Closed Doors.'
'Wild Child.'
'Where Am I?'
'Where There's a Will.'
'Where The Rainbow Ends.'
All available on Amazon in paperback and Kindle

Chapter One

So, here we are again! Those of you who have followed our story so far will be aware of how Steve and I originally met some time ago now, at a time when he was basically hiding away from the world, living rough for a couple of years, running away from the effects of PTSD brought on by a particularly traumatic few years serving as a para, followed by the death of his wife, Beth, son Sean and sister. And then, as if that wasn't enough for any man to deal with, he'd found himself taking me under his wing to help me prove I'd not killed my fiancée! Following a pretty dramatic end to all that he had needed to spend some months in an army rehab centre, until they considered him safe to turn loose on society!

Eventually he was sent back out into my care, assuming that perhaps I could see he didn't relapse into the dangerous state he'd been in previously. I wasn't at all sure I could handle him if he did relapse, but I did know that all I ever truly wanted by then was to be with him, so I agreed to try. I also found myself agreeing to take on the enormous task of bringing about a reunion with his mother and brothers, none of whom he had seen since the funeral of his family, due to his misguided belief that they would have held him responsible for the three deaths. This did actually prove to be the hardest but most rewarding task I had to contend with.

To start with Steve most certainly couldn't face the thought of staying in one place like your average man. Oh no!

He bought a tatty old camper van, got it running (reasonably well), smartened it up, and suggested we go on the road, travelling like a pair of gypsies, just wherever our hearts took us. He even gave this amazing vehicle a name ... he called her Annie van!

During the time we spent just travelling around the country I could tell that he was becoming more and more like the man I'd got to know the previous year, a combination of tough and capable, yet still with a quick sense of humour and quick to poke light hearted fun at me from time to time. Perhaps some people would have taken objection to this, but personally, I loved every minute of it (though I did try hard to look annoyed sometimes, but could never fool him!)

During that first year we had found ourselves travelling from place to place, mostly living as your average homeless folk, sleeping everywhere and anywhere we could. It was during this time that I realised just how deeply Steve felt about the problems faced by others who were in that situation, usually through no fault of their own, and with no way out of it. But it was actually not the first time I had cause to see this in him. That, though I didn't give so much thought to it at the time, was on an occasion when we had cause to lay low in Birmingham for a while during the months he'd been helping me stay out of the hands of the police, or worse still, Jakes killers (Jake was my fiancée). It was on our way back to the pub where we'd managed to acquire some temporary employment to tide us over for our journey. We came across a rather bedraggled looking young lad, apparently having no luck trying to earn money busking. Instead of walking on by as most would do, Steve stopped and spoke to him to find out how he came to be sleeping rough. Having heard enough to know it was down to family problems, Steve got him back on his feet, picked up his guitar and got the lad, Josh, joining in with a brilliant duet! As if that wasn't enough, he then talked the landlord at the pub into taking him on and giving him accommodation to boot! Josh has now become a qualified chef and is working with us! That is just one example of the man Steve Lockett ... the man I'm now proud to say is my husband!

But not to get ahead of myself, during the second year when we went travelling in Annie, I found myself being challenged by Steve to tackle things I would never have contemplated before! He had me trudging up to the summit of Snowdon, swimming in a lake in the Lake District, climbing an absolutely huge climbing wall at a leisure centre run by a mate of his, Chris, and, when I lost my nerve at the top, found myself the sauce of everybody's amusement when Steve had to quite literally peel my hands from the top to get me to abseil back down! He even, with enormous difficulty, dragged me to the top of Scafell Pike.

Oh no, this was certainly no average man; this was Steve Lockett!

As you can tell, boring was not a word applicable to our second year together. We travelled around, sometimes sleeping back to back in our original old sleeping bags from the first year, (well washed by my Mum!), sharing the space provided by the folded down seat and table arrangement in the van. From the time Steve was sent out of rehab I had been warned not to expect more from him than a platonic, almost brotherly, attachment, and so had accepted that just to be close in whatever way possible. Even so, I would often lay there alongside him at nights, listening to his steady breath, and feeling the warmth passing between us in the stillness of night, and just imagine what it would be like to have him love me as much as I knew I loved him. Well, a girl can dream, can't she?

Of course there were many nights when the traumas he had suffered in his past had disturbed him while he slept. I would often hear him shouting, as he would have done to the men he led in battle, to 'get your bloody heads down', and sometimes he would still shout out the name of his wife, Beth, who had been so cruelly killed in that car crash, and I soon realised that any thoughts of complete recovery were too much to hope for. Whether or not, this ever happened, I intended to be there for him as he'd been there for me through my difficult times.

In spite of the serious side of our lives which we were now trying hard to shake off, I got to introduce him to my family, and being somewhat embarrassed when he brought my brother-in-law, Alan, back from a pub more than a little tipsy, and he got to introduce me to his family, not only his mother, May, but also his two brothers. We fitted in visits to my friend Sally who had supported me at a particularly rough patch in our first year, which also led to us introducing her to his youngest brother, Jamie, which in turn brought them to share a double wedding with us later on! It was some time before our marriage that he also took me to meet his, somewhat more serious brother, Tom, his wife Margaret, and girls, Sandra and Tina.

Of course, with Steve, it's hard to go anywhere with him and be sure of just what will happen. It was on the visit to Cambridge to see Sally that Jamie tagged along, and was more than a little shocked by seeing just what happens when someone upsets his brother! We had been heading alongside the river for lunch at a pub there when we came across some louts kicking and abusing an old chap, obviously a rough-sleeper by his dirty, shabby appearance. Steve shouted at them to leave him alone, but one of them just laughed and took another kick at the man, saying that filthy old tramps shouldn't be allowed on the streets! Well, I think I was the only person there who wasn't at all surprised at his next move … Steve grabbed him, called him a few choice words, and dropped him in the river! The others took off, leaving us to take the elderly man with us to the pub for a good hot meal … paid for, I might say, by the other customers who'd been sitting on the veranda and had enjoyed the entertainment.

During Steve's years of army life, he'd apparently spent years training up young recruits and had been accustomed to a strict regime of being wide awake at the crack of dawn, followed by suitable exercises, a brisk jog to work up an appetite! And yes, he did think I should join him! Sometimes I did do my best, but knew it would take years to get anywhere near his level of fitness.

None the less, we genuinely did have so much fun through the early part of the year. For instance, he took great amusement from seeing the embarrassment on people's faces when, seeing us turn up in our tatty old van, people would try to turn us away from something he'd set his mind on. One of these occasions was when we pulled into a yard full of expensive looking cars, intending to hire a long-boat. The owner assumed we were just a pair of travellers, and it was clear he didn't want us there. That was until Steve, flashing his wallet full of cards, gold card included, said not to bother, we'd go elsewhere! Before I could blink we were off down the canal, leaving Annie parked conspicuously next to Roll's, Bentley's and the like!

You see, following his discharge from the army, Steve's money had been going into his account untouched. Then of course, my late fiancée's brother, Andy, had enrolled us both as silent partners in his business in return for Steve capturing Jake's killer, giving us a steady income. On top of that, the house I had shared with Jake in Richmond, had been sold, also adding to our funds.

A similar event to the boat hire was when Steve insisted we go in to a rather posh looking hotel one night for a break from the van. We were both still looking somewhat scruffy and in desperate need of a good clean up! I tried to say no, but he grabbed me firmly by the arm and marched me straight up to the desk, requesting two rooms for the night. Well! If you could have seen the expression on the poor woman's face! Throwing him a look of disgust, she was about to have us escorted out when Steve smiled his best smile at her and just said,

"Are you certain about that Ma'am, you see my sister, Lady Lockett here, is quite exhausted after our travelling?"

Embarrassed as I was, I must admit to seeing the funny side of the sudden change of attitude in her as she allotted us two of her most comfortable rooms that night! The thing with living and travelling about with Steve was that you could never be sure what would happen next. I genuinely didn't care as I knew from day one that I would always be safe if I was with him. And anyway, during the course of that year he had made it his duty to build up my self-confidence by instructing me in the art of self-defence! In fact there were a couple of times in particular when I actually did get the opportunity to put a little of this into good use later!

Up until sometime into our travelling we remained, as you could say, inseparable yet separate, indivisible yet at the same time, individual people. Right from the start I felt that there, by his side, was where I belonged, and to a great extent, I believe he felt a certain security from having me there to share life with. Yes, I know he was physically capable of handling anything that came his way, yet I always believed (or perhaps wanted to believe), that my constant presence and need for his protection gave him back the stimulation he had always gained from his army days of being in control of others.

This was true right up until one particular occasion when, having parked Annie van up to go for a hike, we put down our rucksacks in a clearing to sit by a lake to have a picnic. While Steve turned his hand to unpacking the rug for us to sit on, I wandered toward a weir nearby. There was a little wooden bridge across it, admittedly not a very robust one, but me being me, I couldn't resist walking onto it to watch the fast flowing water passing below. It had been a particularly rainy spell leading up to this, adding to the unusually hard flow escaping below me. Yes ... you can guess what happened next? The bridge gave way, and down I went, swirling down and round out of control, and totally unable to save myself. Of course I needn't have worried, Steve looked round in the nick of time to see what was happening, and the next thing I knew was him, having dived in to rescue me, laying me on the rug, scared and shivering. It was then, after stripping me of my soaking wet clothes and wrapping me in the rug, that he sat with me in his arms to warm me and stop the shaking, and that was when it happened! He turned my face up to his and kissed me so passionately, and then, sensing my reaction to this he lay me down gently and made love to me in the way I'd never dreamt he would! At this point I knew I'd never find another man who could have that effect on me that Steve did that day, and still does so long after.

Ah! Sorry about that; I'm letting my mind wander again! I should be explaining that, not so many minutes after the incident I've just mentioned, it began to rain pretty hard. Knowing we were quite a fair way from the van we decided to follow a small footpath through the woods, and it was then that we came across a large rather ramshackle old house, apparently deserted, and decided to take shelter there. Much to our surprise it was being used by a small group of five people, squatters I suppose you might call them, but wrongly assuming we too were homeless, they had no objections to sharing it with us.

This was the start of a whole new adventure in our lives. The house was called Lansdown Grange, a pretty impressive place back in its day, but by then in a very sorry state. None the less, it didn't take Steve's often over active mind to come up with the urge to find a way to acquire it and convert it into a place to take in those homeless in need of help in one way or another, a sort of posh homeless shelter, you could say!

As it turned out, after a heart-to-heart with his mother about his adoption following her rape, we learnt that the place had actually belonged to the parents of her attacker, Henry Stanwick. Whilst looking through some old photos she had kept showing her parents working as gardener and housekeeper there, an envelope was found which turned out to be the blessing Steve needed. On passing this to a solicitor via his solicitor brother, Tom, it showed that the Stanwick's had left the whole estate to their 'illegitimate' grandson, Steven Lockett, and had at the same time had their son sign over any future rights to the estate in the future!

Although so many believed he was mad to even contemplate what he had in mind, I knew him well enough to know that when Steve got an idea in his head, nothing would stop him. He suggested that, as we already had amongst our new homeless friends squatting there, a builder, a carpenter, a couple who'd lost their small holding/market garden through no fault of their own, shortly joined by a plumber, this would lay the foundation for being able to offer basic training in those skills to any other out of work, homeless folk. The plan was for him (and to a certain extent, me) to work on getting new 'residents' to a good fitness level in mind and body, while they tried their hand at the trades on offer. Then Steve went out and found work or apprenticeships to get them back on their feet and back out into society.

Well, we had our ups and downs, both work wise and on a personal level that year. On a personal level of course, as readers of my last work will recall, I found myself for reasons I couldn't figure out for a while, unsettled and rather neglected by Steve. I felt rather side-lined for some reason. Then gradually, it dawned on me just what it was hiding away in the back of my mind … I'd come to the conclusion I was pregnant! Yes, you probably think I would have been thrilled, but no, I was scared. All I could think of was how drastically hard he'd found it to come to terms with the death of little Sean. And anyway, he'd been so preoccupied lately, and had never shown any sign of wanting any true commitment.

The only person I felt I could talk to at the Grange was Ellen, one of our original residents, who was also pregnant at the time. She said to tell him, but no … I couldn't; so I took off alone didn't I?

This turned out to be a pretty stupid move. It ended with me being captured and held to ransom by Luke Stanwick, son of Henry, in an attempt to force Steve to sign over the place to him. I'm pleased to say his plans came to a quick halt when he and his gang found themselves stopped in their tracks by Steve, with a few mates from a particular 'elite' force he had served with in his time!

Following my return 'home', as I described in my last book, a while later all this was followed up with a most beautiful wedding in June. A day I thought could never be beaten … but then it was. In the middle of January the following year, some two weeks earlier than expected, we became the very proud parents to our little son, Will (William)!! Well, as Steve always said, 'where there's a WILL', and that most certainly proved to be the case.

Chapter Two

As you can imagine, during the years following on from this momentous event, our lives took on a huge change. We were still being kept up to our necks in work developing the Grange into Steve's dream of a shelter cum rehabilitation centre for the homeless, a place where he could help those with no means to acquire the skills needed to gain work to support themselves. In this venture we had been lucky enough to have the help from our permanent residents including Graham, a carpenter, Pete, a builder, Dave, a plumber, and also Bob and his wife Ellen who had had their small holding taken from them to make room for a new road.

With their help and support we had a ready qualified and skilled group to help give less fortunate youngsters chance to try out and, hopefully, decide if any of these trades would be helpful to get them employment, even apprenticeships. We had also been able to employ our young friend Josh, newly qualified as a chef, to work with the help of a young girl called Mia, in the kitchen, to see to the mammoth task of seeing all were suitably fed, an extremely important need to be considered after Steve had driven them almost to drop in his determination to get them fit! This was a man who lived by the theory that a healthy body makes for a healthy mind! Very few excuses were accepted short of old age or illness! On top of this Steve was absolutely unmovable on the rules he laid down. He made these perfectly clear to all those coming to us for assistance. He was as unmovable about this as if the Grange had been an army training camp! Anyone flouting them or believing him to be a soft touch soon learnt their mistake as he gave no second chances. It was a case of, 'one strike and you're out'.

But now there was an added element to our everyday lives, one neither of us had experienced before. The thought of becoming a mother had never crossed my mind until I found myself pregnant. And Steve, though he had fathered young Sean, had been away with his regiment when Sean was born and, due to unforeseen circumstances, had been away on duty until that awful accident on the very day he returned home, which had meant him never getting chance to meet his son whilst he was still alive.

Now here we were, parents, sharing our lives with this amazing little bundle of energy who, right from the first had a way of capturing everyone's hearts. He had arrived a couple of weeks before his due date, showing the same tendency as his father to get on with life and not hang around waiting! He was born with the same dark brown eyes as Steve, with which he would fix all those he saw with an almost hypnotic gaze! In fact, almost from the day he first opened those eyes and looked up at me, I could swear he gave me that same cheeky grin his father had bewitched me with from the day we met! And of course, in the same way as his father, I knew I loved him so much my heart would burst. How can it be possible for a girl like me to have not just one man I loved so much, but now to have yet another smaller, but equally amazing love in my life? Sometimes I would have to sit up during the night just to watch my 'men' sleeping so peacefully, Steve by my side, and Will just across the room in his cot. Sometimes it was all I could do not to lift Will out of his beautifully made wooden cot, hand carved by Graham, just to hold him close.

No, I told myself, it would be wrong to disturb him when he always slept so well right from the start. I knew that we would have to move him into his nursery one day, but for that little while I just felt the need to keep him close by. I don't think I've ever felt as happy as I did right then. After all, what more could a girl want?

Surrounded by so many wonderful people, in particular that group of permanent residents and staff, Will grew into a happy child with a quick smile for anyone who spoke to him. His particular favourite was Ellen's daughter, Lilly. I suppose with only seven months difference in their ages, this was to be expected. We would sit them down on a rug in the garden on a good day, surrounded with toys, and watch as they worked out what to do with them. When we stacked bricks for them it was a rush to see which one got to knock them down first. Whoever did the effect was the same ... hysterical fits of laughter from both!

It wasn't long before Lilly mastered the art of crawling, but despite the difference in age, and obviously not wishing to be outdone, within a couple of weeks Will took everyone by surprise by taking off after her like a pro!

As time went on the two were always to be seen finding new ways to get excitement, not particularly intending to get into mischief, but if that was the outcome it was always Will who was in the lead! Sometimes I couldn't help feeling quite sorry for poor Lilly who would valiantly attempt to shoulder her share of the blame, but as they got to an age that Steve considered sufficient to know right from wrong, I have to say that he would expect his son to be man enough to take the majority of this. This was, as he explained it to me, his father, Peter's way to instil ideas of manly chivalry in him and his brothers! Punishment, if required, was always swift and relevant to the crime. For instance, on one occasion they had been playing around Bob and Ellen's yard. This had by this time been built up into a small farm in part of the land adjoining the Grange. During the course of their games, both being particularly keen on animals of all kinds, they had gone into one sty and had accidently left the door open! By the time Bob found pigs tucking into his freshly dug pile of potatoes, he was not a happy man. He had torn them both off a strip for their carelessness. Lilly was told as punishment she wouldn't be allowed out the next day, but when Steve heard what had happened he had not only given eight year old Will a good talking to, but, in spite of Bob insisting it wasn't necessary, had stood over his son while the lad mucked out all three sty's single handed! As he told him, responsibility is a lesson best learnt early to prevent problems throughout life.

I suppose to some this must sound as if he was perhaps rather harsh on our beloved son, but this was certainly not the case. It was clear that his father, his adoptive father, Peter, had brought him up with the same sense of responsibility, especially as the eldest of three boys, so he was never unnecessarily harsh so much as just firm with Will. In fact, though nobody but me would have known, having to punish Will in any way would often upset him more than he'd let on, but he was determined to see to it that his son should share his same values.

Of course, it was surprising to find that Will ever found time to get up to much mischief. By the time he was six years old he insisted on following Steve onto the front lawn each morning for what was now a compulsory exercise session for all those capable of doing so. Small as he was, it was amusing to see the small figure standing alongside the tall, muscular body of his father, making his best attempt at copying every move, be it stretch, star jump, or running on the spot! I would have to be on hand at that point to drag him away, somewhat reluctantly I must say, as there was no way he could join the jog around the estate, and besides which it was time to get ready for school.

Even from an early age Will was somewhat dismissive of the benefits of that establishment, almost to the point of me considering home schooling. After all, I'd been lucky enough to have had a very good education myself, and felt sure I could get him a good grounding on most subjects, but I knew that the social interaction he'd get by going to the school in the village would be important. And of course, I could still be there to help and encourage him with anything he didn't understand (though being cautious not to let him rely on me for answers, just for suggestions).

Another advantage to him getting to know the village kids was that Steve had recently been persuaded to take over the local scouts with me coping with the cubs, meaning that Will was automatically enrolled in each in turn as he got to the appropriate age. I seriously think he originally expected, as Dad was in charge, that this would mean he would not have to put in so much effort to progress through both these groups, but he soon was put right on that count! Steve made it his duty to show no favouritism to any, not even his own son.

Chapter Three

By now Lansdown Grange had seen considerable change since we first took it over. What was once an extremely neglected old Victorian mansion, had now been completely refurbished and was now an elegant building, mainly thanks to our assortment of skilled residents. The grounds around it too had been transformed into unrecognizable perfection, with carefully manicured lawns, clipped box hedges, and flower beds ablaze with colours.

Steve, Will and I had an apartment upstairs in the left wing of the house, while the right wing was mostly divided into two dormitories; one for the men and one for women. The majority of those using these tended to be reasonably temporary.

Behind the main house there had been a magnificent stable block, but this had been transformed into four large and comfortable bungalows for our more permanent residents. By this time Bob and Ellen had moved into one of the lodge cottages to place them at a suitable distance between the garden, which was in their keeping, and the small piece of farm land just outside the perimeter. This was now their domain on which to grow food and rear livestock, teaching those skills to those with an interest, whilst helping to provide food for us all. More often than not they would have an abundance of goods which they could sell to local shops or individuals, even after providing plenty to Josh and Mia for the kitchen.

As Steve's main aim with the Grange was to provide help for the homeless, amongst which there was always a small number of ex-military, there was a need for more accommodation than the original buildings supplied, but this was soon remedied by adding another array of small separate lodges paid for partly by the grant we had managed to acquire, and partly with a small part of the legacy left in the will by the late Mrs Stanwick, (Steve's Grandmother, and mother to rapist, Henry Stanwick). Of course, having lived rough himself for just over two years, Steve had needed to learn quickly just how to survive this sort of life, and had soon come to realise the problems which drove others into that situation. In these days when redundancy was rife in some areas, there were, and still are, many finding themselves unable to keep up payments on either rented properties or mortgages. In such dire cases this left far too many being evicted and left homeless. Though local authorities would attempt to find accommodation, this was often only temporary and of a very low standard.

Most tried hard to regain employment, but most employers would only consider those with some sort of skills, and even then they needed a permanent home address to be taken on. Obviously this became, and still is, a vicious circle … no address, no job; no job, no money to pay rent!

And then, as ex-para Steve was well aware from his own experience, those coming back into civilian life from the forces had even bigger hills to climb! This new world to them found them in what is almost an alien environment, one they are often ill-equipped for. As with Steve, most of these are intelligent, skilful people in what they do, but finding the right niche to slot into outside of the life they've lived for a good few years, does not come easy. On top of that, as he was well aware from his own experience, many, like Steve, came home suffering from the effects of PTSD, leaving them in need of even more care.

With all of this being a matter which Steve, as it should be with us all, has always been keen to help find ways to deal with, it was having the Grange project which became his salvation in so many ways. It gave him a true purpose to focus on, one where he could utilise all his talents. Not only did he take firm control of the organisation needed to turn this into a thriving business whilst still developing it as an extremely grand homeless shelter, but threw himself whole heartedly into working to encourage those who came to us to find ways to help themselves, be it with the (often pretty intense) fitness classes he ran on a daily basis, plus for those with no particular skills, the opportunity to pick up the basics of bricklaying, plumbing, carpentry, or even those of basic farming or gardening. As long as they, especially the younger ones, put their effort into helping themselves, he would put all his effort into helping them build some sort of new life for themselves. The fact that they could apply giving an address at Lansdown Grange meant that, with the reputation Steve had built up for the place, employers tended to look much more favourably on them. Though some stayed for some time, many passed through our hands over fairly quickly when they found steady work which was sufficient to support themselves in rented accommodation.

In fact one of the most rewarding things was when they came back to visit and update us on how their new lives were going. Of course, the very first of these was a young lad by the name of Jez who had been here squatting with the others when we first found the place. He had been doing a sports science degree but had dropped it half way through following the breakup of his parents' marriage. With much, particularly firm, pushing from Steve, he had managed not only to get his body back into full fitness, but been encouraged to motivate himself sufficiently to re-claim a place on his course. He had completed his degree and was now fully qualified. In fact I firmly believe that it was his success with turning this lads life around that had a lot to do with keeping Steve determined to push so hard to make his plans come to fruition.

Seeing so many different people pass through our care here never ceased to be rewarding. To see some of the youngsters arrive here looking almost beyond help and beyond hope, and watch them as they gradually learn to accept the help on offer to turn themselves around, was such a gratifying experience.

In fact by this time Lansdown Grange had become known as the 'come to' place for employers needing apprentices or workers, both skilled or with a good basic grounding in the necessary jobs they needed to fill. They knew that those they took on would work to their best ability, and even more important, would be reliable. Given jobs to go to they knew that this was too good an opportunity to turn down, and that if they let Steve down, he would never consider having them back. The principal of this being a one-time chance of rescue from their predicament meant that the majority were glad to accept the help on offer. Of course there were exceptions made on rare occasions when Steve could see he had paired the wrong person with an unsuitable job, but he was a pretty good judge on these matters, but in such a case he was never too proud to admit his mistake, take that person back, and try again.

As I have already stated, there was always a number of ex-military who would find their way to us. Some came home to find that their families, often their wives, had moved on, or that they just felt they no longer fitted in to the lives they'd left. Some, like Steve, had problems with PTSD, and found this was something they needed a great deal of help to overcome (or at the very least, to come to terms with).

Although I'd achieved a psychology degree at university, this by no means qualified me to give the level of help needed in their cases. You may remember (those who read about Steve's rehabilitation provided by the army), that he was well supervised by a particularly good counsellor by the name of Paul Wilkie. We kept in regular touch with him, which of course we had been asked to do when we first set off on our wanderings. Well, by the time Will reached two years old, Paul couldn't resist visiting, curious to see just what a mini Steve was like I believe! Whilst staying for a few days he was so impressed with what we'd achieved here that, when we explained how many ex-military we found requesting places here, without hesitation he offered to take up the position of official counsellor! It seemed he had served his time as an army counsellor and was keen to move on to pastures new, and he felt our pastures might just fit the bill! Of course we welcomed him with open arms. At least, I thought with a secret laugh, Will is living proof that he was wrong when he warned me not to expect more than 'brotherly' love from Steve!

Having Paul join our team proved a great asset as he had plenty of experience and an easy manner which put people very much at their ease. I clearly remember one young man in particular who we were struggling to communicate with just before Paul came. The lad had been keen to join a local football team, but for assorted reasons which were nothing to do with lack of ability, had not achieved this. He'd found himself drifting in and out of different jobs, none of which felt right, and consequently ended up out of work and homeless, with no clue what to do or where to go next. This led to him feeling a deep resentment for life in general and blaming everyone else for all that had happened to him. By the time Steve had given him a good talking to about the need to get fit and refocus, and Paul had worked with him to help him believe in himself and realise life wasn't out to get him, he took it into his head to apply to join the RAF, and was accepted immediately. I believe it was Steve and Paul who between the two of them had restored the young man's confidence in his own ability.

Of course, as you can guess, Paul soon became firm friends with young William. The feeling was mutual of course. Over the years since Paul had joined us Will quickly learnt how to wrap Paul around his little finger, though I don't think this went entirely unnoticed by Paul. It seemed that Paul, not being the marrying type, had obviously had no children of his own, and thoroughly enjoyed spending time with Will being shown all his 'secret places' around the grounds. On one occasion I went out looking for him with no luck until, giving up the search and heading back through the woods, I heard a distinctive, though barely audible, giggle. I stopped and looked around me, assuming this would be Will and Lilly hiding behind the undergrowth, but when it came again I realised the sound was, as suspected, Will, but not from behind the undergrowth, or with Lilly; no, somehow he had persuaded Paul to climb up onto a branch of a large chestnut tree, and though it clearly amused Will to see me hunting for him, poor Paul was hanging onto a branch looking somewhat less than confident ... actually, more like scared. Of course I tried very hard not to laugh as I waited while Will ran to fetch Pete with a ladder and watched him peel poor Paul off the branch he was hanging on to!

I really did try to scold the boy for his actions that day, but I don't think I did a very good job of keeping a straight face.

Chapter Four

As I mentioned previously, Steve had been bombarded with requests to take on the running of the local scout group. At first he had refused, saying that he was used to training soldiers, not small boys! Nether the less, the requests kept coming. The people in the nearby villages had got to see the positive effect he'd had on the assorted waifs and stray (as they saw them), pretty well always being able to turn them around to make good citizens, and they could see he would have a good influence on their children. Of course, when he first got persuaded to undertake the task he hadn't realised that now, unlike when he was a kid, this would be a mixture of boys and girls! Then of course there was also the younger ones, the cubs.

In the end he had been persuaded to take on the scouts on condition that I took on the cubs. This I was quite happy to do, enlisting Paul to back me up. I felt I could manage the eight to ten year old children with no problem. In my innocence I truly thought that, being so young, this would be a cushy job … how wrong could I be?

Having grown up in a fairly relaxed and happy family where, being so much younger than my sister, I rarely had cause to argue and fight with siblings, and the school I went to being particularly strict on behaviour, but it soon became clear that there were certain disruptive elements in my group of cubs! I have to admit that our Will often turned out to be the ring leader if there was any mischief going on though. Of course, this meant that I had to be seen clamping down on him pretty hard or I'd not have kept the respect of the parents, or control of their children.

The real favourite pastime for my troop was, as you might guess, the evenings when we would sit round a camp fire toasting marshmallows, or waiting for foil wrapped potatoes to bake in the hot ashes around the base of the fire.

A number of times during the year we would have a weekend camp. With the cubs this was always in the grounds of the Grange. If the weather was against us putting up tents this would be transferred to the big barn which, after much effort over time, we had renovated to the standard needed to hire out for weddings, parties, and assorted other occasions.

The barn had proved to be a great asset to our business, bringing in a good amount to support our basic work. It also gave the residents (those we took in) chance to serve a useful purpose, whilst at the same time impressing outsiders with showing off their skills. It was rewarding to see how often those coming in to use our facilities would chat to some, especially younger unemployed folk, and on occasions would hand them cards, asking them to go along for an interview of some sort.

Going back to the cubs, it was just one of these weekends, when we were having an 'indoor' camp in the barn that Paul had gone back indoors to find the supplies I'd left ready. He seemed a long time, so I went after him, making the pack promise to be on their best behaviour. Needless to say this proved to be a complete disaster! While we were gone someone (naming no names!) decided it would be a good idea to rush outside, collect an armful of brushwood, and light a fire in the middle of the barn, intending to cook sausages on it when they arrived!

By the time we came back the place was full of smoke, and flames were beginning to rise to a horrifying height! Luckily we always kept a couple of water troughs either side of the doors for such an event. Paul grabbed a bucket and started tackling the fire while I ushered all the children out into the rain and herded them to the house. By this time Paul had sounded the fire alarm in the barn, and Steve had turned out with a number of men to help get things under control.

As it turned out, it was more smoke damage than anything else, and though I tried to take the blame by saying I'd left them alone for a short time, Steve was fuming! He came straight back into the dining room where I had the kids recovering with hot drinks and biscuits, marched straight past me and tore into them in a way you might expect if these were grown men, but these were all between eight to ten years old. By the time he stopped and asked whose idea it had been, most of them were either in tears or not far from it!

At this point he looked across at me and saw my expression.

"Ok, but you must all see how dangerous that was? I didn't want to upset you but neither did I want to upset your parents by having to send them all to the hospital to find you now, did I? Just tell me though, just which one of you decided to do this?"

I winced, knowing as I did who was usually the ring leader. The room went quiet, no one wanting to place the blame. I was pretty sure this culprit would keep quiet, and that that would not sit well with Steve to think that one amongst them was too cowardly to take the blame.

I was so wrong of course. Will (rather sheepishly) stepped forward, looked up at his father, and admitted to thinking it would be 'helping' with the cooking! I stood there holding my breath for a minute, not knowing just what reaction to expect form Steve who was looking down at his small son in the way I'd have expected if this had been an army recruit. Of course I needn't have worried, the next expression that briefly flashed across his face told me that he was proud of Will ... not for starting the fire, but for having the nerve to own up to doing so knowing he'd most certainly be suitably punished.

"Right young man. Seven o'clock tomorrow I want you down the barn with the men, sweeping, scrubbing and whatever else it takes to undo the damage you've caused, do you understand?"

Oh how I'd wished I'd had a camera in my hand to record the way that was said, and even more so the immediate response of,

"Yes Sir," from son to father!

Anyway, that night all were well fed by Josh, and bedded down in the main hall. I truly think that it was the effect of the way Steve had laid into them all that meant that my cub troop suddenly became so much easier to control!

Meanwhile I think Steve was really finding the older scouts truly rewarding. Sort of 'mini soldiers', was how he looked on them! He would take them on long treks out in the country, sometimes using our mini bus plus any available parents to transport them to places further afield.

One place which always went down well was of course, his mate Chris's activity centre, where he'd taken me so long ago. Back then, you may remember if you read my earlier efforts, this was where he pestered me to climb to the top of a huge climbing wall (well, it seemed huge to me!), but made me the laughing stock of the place when I froze at the top and he had to climb up and quite literally peel me off! You'll be perhaps surprised to hear that I've now at least mastered the smaller ones. Of course all the youngsters absolutely love it there. As well as the walls, Chris has now added a skate park and a carting track.

But it seemed that whatever activities Steve put before them, they were always eager to try, and all had complete trust in him. I believe they would have followed him anywhere he chose to take them. Even after so many years away from his profession in the paras it was so ingrained in him to command respect and discipline that he was still getting just that, only from a troop of scouts!

Whilst Paul and I would sometimes take our cubs to the local swimming pool, Steve took it into his head to be more adventurous with the scouts. Having insisted that those keen to join him should first acquire wet suits, he spent a number of weekends taking them camping in the lake district, and teaching them the technicalities of swimming safely in the relatively cold water of the lakes, just as he had with me all those years ago. I often took Will along to watch, but plead as he might, there was no way his father would allow him to join them until he considered him old enough to cope with the strength and endurance it took to do so. So I soon found a solution which kept both father and son happy!

Whilst Steve swam alongside the scouts to encourage and instruct them, Will and I found that we could hire kayaks and paddle alongside. By the time we started to do this he was nearly old enough to move up and join Steve's scouts. This put him in the lucky position of being able to go either on the water, or in it, depending on what Steve had lined up each time. Of course, as you would expect, the Lansdown scouts were run pretty much as a mini-army training group! Obviously Steve had spent so much of his youth working up to join the army, and then spent so long actually in the parachute regiment, that this was the only way he knew to run it, but during all the time he did I don't believe I ever heard of one single scout, be it girl or boy, complain. Oh yes, there was always the odd grumble or two about how hard he worked them, but for all that they still kept coming, and were always sorry when they had to leave to put time into school, college or university.

I was always concerned that I didn't have his ability to bring the younger ones on to be prepared for Steve's discipline. In particular I must admit, knowing our lad as I did, that I was just a little concerned that with me not having been quite as strict with my cubs as he was with the scouts, Steve might find Will a disrupting influence, but I needn't have worried on that score. Since the rollicking he received from his father over the fire in the barn, he knew now that misbehaviour of any sort would not be tolerated (or certainly if it happened in view of his father!). Ok, I wouldn't claim him to have been a perfect angel, but he was quick to learn not to get caught. In fact, on one of his Nanny May's visits I asked what Steve had been like at Will's age. She assured me that he had been exactly the same as Will, and she often had to cover for him to his father, Peter. It seems Peter had been equally strict with his three sons, especially Steve being eldest. As she explained, if any of them misbehaved, and worse still answered him back, he would never use any form of corporal punishment, but would just withdraw privileges to make his point. I gather this always had the right affect.

May was always so pleased to see Will as he grew up. As she said, it was like having Steve all over again. As she said to me when we were alone one day, after the way he'd lost little Sean, she was so pleased to see the bond they had built. Things could have been so different between them, but as it turned out seeing the two, father and son, together, was always a great source of satisfaction to all who knew them, but none so much as May and myself.

We had seen Steve go from being a wreck of a man, to being such a well-balanced and loving father. And we had got such fun from watching young Will, from the age of barely six, out on the front lawn alongside his tall, fit looking father, in the early morning exercise sessions he ran for those residents in need of motivation, attempting star jumps, push ups etc., and watched as the two grew ever closer and more alike.

Consequently it was not surprising to me to see our boy, by the age of barely fifteen achieve the honour of becoming the area junior champion for clay pigeon shooting, followed later on at the age of eighteen by gaining a black belt in both judo and taekwondo, obviously all taught by Steve as he insisted he needed to see this was done properly. Along with actually learning the different techniques, he was insistent that Will should also learn the discipline to control how these were used. As he told the lad, he was only teaching him these as a competition sport, definitely not for fighting! Although not to the same level, Steve had also spent time with Lilly and some of the other youngsters living at the Grange teaching them self-defence techniques in the same way he had me, as he rubbed into them, this was purely for protection, and never to be used to attack anybody.

Even so, there was just one occasion when we had gone into town for an evening out and had come out of a restaurant just in time to find our local constable, Jim, doing his best to separate two lads from a fight. One of them was one of our temporary homeless who Steve had been helping look for work. They were both quite big lads, far too much for Jim to deal with alone, and just as I knew what would happen, Steve stepped forward,

"Ok Jim, I've got this,"

And of course that's just what happened. He stepped forward, almost between them, taking each by the collar on their shirts, bashed their heads together (ouch! I could feel it from where I stood), and bellowed at the village lad to get off home! The other one he marched briskly back to our car, threw him in the back seat, and drove home in silence. I could feel the rage coming from him like the heat from a boiler.

I wondered what he would do or say when we arrived. Actually I felt he was livid enough to have beaten the youngster up, but of course that wasn't his style. No; as soon as he parked up he practically dragged the boy from the car and told him to get to bed,

"And I want you in my office at six-thirty in the morning. Do you understand me?"

I actually found myself feeling quite sorry for the lad because I knew whatever was coming in the morning wouldn't be pleasant.

When the morning came I did wonder if the lad would actually have the nerve to face Steve, but then I knew that if he didn't it would be all the worse for him. As I was coming down the stairs that next morning I met the boy coming toward me, looking particularly sheepish I must say, and as he came nearer he asked in a hushed voice,

"Do you know what'll happen Mrs Lockett? Is he going to throw me out?"

I could truthfully tell him that I had no idea. One thing I'd learnt over the years about Steve was that when his temper was up it was best to wait until it cools down, pretty much as it was best not to touch a boiling kettle, but to wait for the heat to die down!

"But whatever it is, you were told not to go fighting and learn to behave. You do know he almost had a job lined up for you, don't you? There's every chance you've blown that. The best you can hope for is that you don't find yourself back on the streets before the days out. Now I suggest you get up there a bit sharp, apologise, if he'll listen that is, and take whatever he says like the man you thought you were last night!"

With the briefest of hesitations he turned away from me, shot up the stairs two at a time (the hall clock had just struck six-thirty), and knocked nervously on the door of Steve's office. I couldn't help thinking as I watched the nervous way he went in it was a bit like entering a lion's den for the lad!

It seemed Steve had the perfect punishment ... not just for this lad, but the village one as well. As neither agreed to which one of them had started it, Steve first called in Will to take over the morning exercise session, then drove to the village with the lad. He marched up to the home of the other culprit and knocked. Once he explained to the lads' father, he was quite happy for his son to take the same punishment. It seemed he was dragged from his bed and, without time for breakfast, pushed out to join Steve who then took them both on a gruelling five mile jog, barely slowing from his usual pace to allow for their lack of fitness!

By the time they got almost back he directed them to his car, armed each with a sack, a litter picker and some small plastic bags, before jogging round into the small park in the centre of the village. Here he sat himself on a bench and watched as they went round filling the sacks with litter.

Some of the village kids were curious and came to see what they were doing, and it was then that the village lad asked Steve,

"So what do we do with these?" holding up the small bags.

Well, I wish I'd have seen his face when Steve, trying hard not to roar with laughter said,

"Oh those; they're to pick up the dog muck you've just stood in lad!"

It seems that the on looking kids enjoyed the joke too. Regardless off that Steve would not allow either of them to stop until he was satisfied with the results, and convinced they'd both learnt a valuable lesson.

Even so, though he allowed the lad to stay at the Grange realising he was obviously still in need of a firm hand and guidance, he did overlook him for the warehouse job he'd lined up for him promising him to keep him in mind when he felt he could be trusted.

When he got home that morning I overheard Will ask his father two questions;

"Why didn't you just give him a good hiding, and then kick him back out where he came from?"

Steve's answer to these was typical of the man I knew so well.

"No son; humiliation works far better than showing him that aggression is the only answer. And as for kicking him out, what good would it do without giving him a chance to learn to be a better man first?"

Chapter Five

Being able to do so off the roads and around the estate, by the time Will was not much past sixteen he had already been able to get to grips with driving our old Annie van, meaning that as soon as he turned seventeen he was well ready to take his driving test. Steve had decided that we should buy him a good, reliable little second hand car to get to grips with in plenty of time before taking him out of the estate and onto the public roads (after all, Annie was beginning to show her age), and though he would have liked something more showy and speedy, he was grateful not to have to be seen doing his test in a camper van! His friend Lilly had taken two attempts, but he was certain he'd do it in one. As he went off that morning with his father by his side he had a real air of confidence, telling me I'd be able to cut up his 'L' plates when he got back. As it turned out though, his confidence was a little short lived when he set off with the certainty of passing first time, just to find that sometimes pride comes before a fall! Being so sure of himself on this occasion proved to be his downfall when he found himself having to make an emergency stop when a dog ran across the road in front of him. Though he should have been prepared for the unexpected, this time he was obviously not, and as a consequence found he had stalled the engine! Never mind … at least he missed the poor dog and learnt by his mistake not to be so sure of himself, and that he needed to put in a little more concentration next time.

During this time though he had been struggling with the problem of just what to do with his life once he'd finished school. He agonised over this for practically all of his last years of education. He considered some sort of sports science degree as our young Jez had done, but that didn't really appeal. In fact, and this was what I'd been absolutely dreading, his main idea for some time was to follow in his father's footsteps and apply to join the army, with a view to getting into the paras. As soon as he mentioned this idea to me I felt my heart sink as I already felt I knew what Steve's reaction to this would be.

I said nothing about it to him, hoping the idea would be short lived, but one particular evening as we sat together I found myself being too slow to change the subject when Steve turned to Will and asked directly,

"Well son, have you decided yet what you want to do. I know you ruled out sports science, but you must have some other idea by now surely? You can't leave it much longer you know or you won't get a place at university."

"That's ok Dad, I don't think I need to go to uni for what I want to do."

Steve looked up from the computer with a look mixed between curiosity and relief on his face,

"Well, come on then, just what is it you've decided that doesn't need any further education. Are you planning on running off to join the circus?"

"No Dad, what I'm thinking of isn't quite that silly!"

I held my breath at that point as I guessed what bombshell he was about to drop. And on top of that I was pretty sure I knew the sort of reaction to expect if I was right.

"Well, spit it out then Will. Just what is it you think you could do that would need no degree?"

Poor lad; there he was so full of enthusiasm at his chosen path ahead, but certainly not expecting the reaction it was to bring about.

"I'm thinking of enlisting in the army and hoping I can make it into the paras like you did. What do you think Dad?"

Steve stopped what he was doing and stood up. For a prolonged second or two neither of us said a word ... I didn't know what to say, and it was clear that Steve was shaken to the core at Will's revelation. I was about to attempt a few pacifying words and a change of subject, but it was too late. Steve came round from behind his desk, took hold of Will and, shaking him as he did so, yelled at the boy,

"You can get that bloody idea out of your mind! There's absolutely no way that's going to happen. Do you hear me?

And getting a very shocked nod of acknowledgement from his son, Steve stormed out of the room and down the stairs. We heard the front door slam behind him!

When Will found his voice to speak again he looked round at me and said,

"Wow! What was that about Mum? I thought he'd be pleased I wanted to follow him. Seems I got that one well wrong."

It was clear that Steve would not come back until he'd calmed down, and so I took the opportunity to sit Will down and explain the whole story to him. I think Steve had always avoided speaking to him about this before, but I knew that now was the time he needed to understand.

I felt so sorry for the poor lad at that point. I knew he'd genuinely meant it when he said that this was his first choice of career, but then he hadn't been around to see the old Steve, the one who had spent two years living rough to escape the terrible effects of PTSD he had suffered following his lengthy service in the parachute regiment. Of course, this had been made worse by the terrible loss of his family on their way to meet him. And, as if that wasn't enough to tear the poor man to pieces, we had then been confronted with his nemesis, the ex-sergeant who he knew had been responsible for the cold blooded murder of a young recruit! It was hardly surprising therefore that he was determined to keep his beloved son safe from such things.

Will sat there absolutely speechless, listening almost in disbelief. Had it been anyone else who'd told him the story I doubt he would have believed it. As far as he was concerned there was no one he looked up to more than his father, and now he knew so much more about Steve's background I believe this was doubly so. I could tell there were so many questions he wanted to ask, but just then couldn't get his head around it all.

"It's not your fault Will, you were not to know how he felt. I suppose I should have warned you, but I thought you'd decided against that for a career. I you very disappointed dear?"

And then thought I should ask, "Will you still want to do that, or have you any other ideas?"

I believe I just may have had my fingers crossed behind my back as I asked this question, but heaved a sigh of relief when he put a hand on my arm and said,

"After what you've just told me I think not, don't you? There's plenty of other ideas I can choose from after all."

"And you're not too disappointed then?"

He put his arms round me, gave me a much appreciated hug, and assured me that, seeing what the army had done to his father, there was no way he wanted to entertain the idea. Yes, he was as tough (well, nearly!) as Steve, but had been brought up to be a gentle and considerate young man, and somehow I couldn't see him being put in a position of having to fight anyway.

When Steve did come back in I could tell he was still feeling pretty upset, partly because of what Will had said to him, but mostly because of the way he'd spoken to his son. I was about to step in and find a way to repair the damage between them when, to my utter surprise, in that casual and matter of fact way youngsters have sometimes, Will turned to his father and said,

"Hey Dad, I've decided to go with my other idea and do something totally different,"

We both turned to look at him, wondering what revelation to expect next,

"What do you think my chances are of getting a business and management degree? Then perhaps I can come back and help you out later ... you know; when you're too old to cope!"

And he was just quick enough to duck the swipe coming in a friendly way from Steve!

"Cheeky young git! How old do you think I am? I'll still be running this place for a good many years after you struggle through that one. But yes, it would be a useful degree to have I reckon. It would give you scope to get into a good choice of employment later if you chose not to come back here to work with us. You'd better have words with the career adviser at school to see what they think your chances are."

Though neither noticed me in the background, I couldn't help heaving a great sigh of relief. Knowing we were all back on an even keel again was a big comfort. After all, other than the odd little hiccup along the way, the three of us had lived in reasonable harmony all these years, and that's how I liked it!

Over the next two years we watched our son really get his head down and study with real determination. We watched as he achieved top marks with his GCSE exams, followed by equally good marks in the subjects he chose for A Levels.

Knowing he would be going off to study at Coventry University, though I knew this wasn't so very far from home, like all mothers must be when their young fly the nest, I spent weeks shopping and ensuring, not so much for him as myself, that he had all he needed to feel comfortable and well catered for in all possible respects! Steve kept telling me to stop fussing and allow the boy to grow up, but somehow I felt unable to let go as easily as he did. Not that Steve wanted to get rid of him, but he could see more easily than me that this was Will's time to grow from a boy to a man. Ok … I knew he was right and that I had to let him go (and just pray he'd come back one day!).

Chapter Six

So there we were, back to where we started eighteen years ago, just the two of us again. Well, that wasn't exactly accurate; we have never been just the two of us since that first day that we walked into the derelict Lansdown Grange, met our small group of homeless squatters, each with their own skills but no way to find work and no homes, and then, for reasons explained in my previous writing, finding that Steve had actually inherited the place from the deceased owners!

Having lived rough for a good two years, Steve could see the potential immediately and, having added the rest of his inheritance to the grant we were able to get, and with the skills of the others to pull it round, we'd spent these years running this as a centre to take in, re-train and rehome so many others in need of help. And now we had also spent the last eighteen years raising our amazing son here. I'd watched lovingly as he grew into a smaller, younger version of his father, and now he'd gone.

All of our original residents, those who had been more than glad to stay with us and pass on a little of their knowledge to those who came in off the streets with no previous training for any occupation, were obviously that bit older now, as were we, but none too old to put effort into showing off their skills in the hope that some of the youngsters might decide to try their hand at similar work when such was available.

In these invaluable assistants we had a plumber (Dave), a carpenter (Graham), a builder (Pete), and of course the invaluable Bob and Ellen, parents of Will's friend Lilly, who were now in total charge of the small market garden which provided food for us all plus some to sell on, and also worked hard with any help available to maintain the immaculate gardens surrounding the main house. This meant that we always had the perfect setting for taking bookings for weddings, conferences and other functions. These were normally held either in the grounds or in the large barn (the one Will had nearly set light to so long ago!).

One other big asset we had of course was in having our own well qualified, and now well experienced chef in Josh. Working in the kitchen with Mia, they not only did the catering for all those living here, all the catering for any events taking place here, but also took a number of youngsters under their wings to learn the catering trade.

With all of this in mind we had managed to turn around so many lives over our time here. So many who would otherwise most probably have ended up spending so long homeless, and therefore out on the streets, many no doubt ending eventually turning to drugs and drink to wipe their misery from their minds.

This was all Steve's aim from that very first day, and he had taken the unfortunate circumstances of his birth, added this to the pain he'd suffered before we started our journey together, and had now proved to the doubters that good can come out of bad if just one person put their mind to doing this.

Now Will had moved on and for a while I felt empty inside, almost like everlasting hunger pangs. But then I soon realised this was natural for any mother. Once I stopped feeling sorry for myself for what I'd lost, I turned back to see what (or who) I did still have ... Steve of course! When I looked back to the time when he had helped me through my nightmare months, and then that first year when we'd broke away from everyone to go travelling in our old Annie van, ending up here, where we now call home, what more could I want than my Steve?

I had no idea just how life would be from now on, but I was sure it would never be dull. It seemed that our work at Lansdown Grange was becoming known much further afield than we ever expected. At first when we began our work we were just a part of a smaller community, but news travels fast, and we were getting requests to travel around, first the local area, and then much further afield, giving talks to all and sundry about our work. But now, as time went on, this first rush of interest had slowed and offers of help had begun to wane. Funds were gradually becoming tight.

Before we knew it Will's two years was up, and he returned home triumphant, degree in hand, and announced that he felt the need to take a gap year! Steve wasn't over impressed when his son announced that he was intent on travelling before settling into a job, and even less impressed when he heard that Lilly had agreed to go with him! She hadn't chosen to go to university, just to a local agricultural and horticultural college to study. Since then she had just been working alongside her parents.

Of course, when Steve tried to show his objection to the whole plan, Will was quick to point out that at his age his father has been all over the world with the army, he just felt the need to widen his horizons before settling down to an occupation. Secretly I couldn't help thinking that he needed to find his own way to prove himself to his father and not get tied down to life in an office environment too soon.

"And anyway, Lilly would really enjoy travelling too, and you know her parents wouldn't let her roam off on her own. At least she'd be safe with me, wouldn't she?"

Steve, trying hard to keep a grin from spreading across his face, turned to look Will straight in the face and in his most serious tone of voice said,

"Well ok. But first you clear it with Bob and Ellen. Then just you promise me that she will be safe, not just with you, but safe from you too!" He caught his son's eye, and for a minute, held his gaze, "Do you understand what I mean lad?"

Obviously feeling somewhat embarrassed, Will nodded his head vigorously and assured Steve that they were just going as good friends that was all.

"After all Dad, she's always been like a sister to me hasn't she?"

And so, two weeks later, we stood alongside Bob and Ellen, waving goodbye to our offspring as they set off in a taxi, bound for the airport and their 'big adventure'. Where they had planned to go first, so we were told, was across to Europe with a plan to work their passage down, eventually in the hope of reaching India, perhaps even Australia or New Zealand, but we'd agreed to give them free rein and trust in their common sense to keep them safe. Only time (and perhaps the odd postcard) would tell!

Chapter Seven

Over the next few months we barely heard from our two wanderers. We did get a brief text from Will four days after their departure, but this told us very little, just that "all's ok, will be in touch again later", and then nothing for ages!

A couple of weeks later came another one, this time from Lilly to her parents, just saying that they had found a few weeks work in a small hotel somewhere down in the south of France, but nothing more explicit than that. Steve was all for texting Will back and warning him not to get led into drinking, but I told him in no uncertain terms that he really must let go of the reins and trust our boy! Somewhat reluctantly he agreed.

Somehow I believe I really thought their plans were pretty ambitious, but knew Will would never truly settle down without first exploring what else there was out there to see. Though I said little of my opinion to Steve, I did find it easy to talk to Ellen about my views and any concerns on the couple, sort of mother to mother, as it were. The feeling that she was so happy to entrust her daughter's safety to our Will was good. I had wondered if he had press-ganged her into the whole idea, but from what Ellen said it seemed it had been as much Lilly who had at first suggested it.

The next we heard from them was not until about a month later when they sent a postcard showing a magnificent view across the Mediterranean Sea, taken from a beach in Crete.

There was no explanation as to how they got there, or where they were heading next!

I quite expected them to be writing or messaging at any time to ask for help with funds to survive, but that never happened. I know they had planned to work their way as they went, but us mothers had joked about just how long it would be before this plan fizzled out and we had a desperate call for help in that department. I didn't voice this thought to Steve though, in fact I was careful not to even hint at the possibility as we were finding our own funds were beginning to dry up.

Though he wouldn't admit it, every time I glanced unexpectedly when he was working at his desk, I couldn't help catching a glimpse of worry on his face which he would change into a smile as soon as he saw me looking his way. When I tried to discuss the finances of the Grange with him he would brush it aside with a joke or two about me not having much of a head for figures, and that there was nothing much to worry about. It was the 'nothing much' that I could tell was causing him to look particularly haggard on occasions.

Eventually, about ten months after leaving home, we were just having breakfast when there was a sound coming from the office which took us a second or two to recognise.

"Oh quick, go and answer it."

Steve, being nearer than me, dashed through to find it was Will and Lilly on Skype!

"Good evening folks. How's things there in the rain? The news says you've been getting wet lately!"

"What do you mean, 'good evening'? We've just had breakfast. So where the hell are you then? Thought it was next stop India?"

"Well, it was going to be but we had a change of direction and found ourselves in Oz instead."

By then I'd come to join the conversation. It seemed they changed their minds, not wanting to be gone too long to see Australia before coming home. Steve asked what they were doing to earn money to live on, and Will explained they'd been able to apply for a temporary visa which allowed them to go fruit picking for a few weeks, but as this would soon run out they thought it would be the right time to come home.

I couldn't help being amused when he told us that they'd found a way to get fed on the cheap. It seemed that, whilst in a bar somewhere out in the wilds Will had been challenged by one of the locals to a dual ... not with fighting, but on guitar! Apparently some chap had thrown a guitar at him and bet he couldn't out play him. Little did he know that this was another skill he'd learnt from his father years ago! All the locals put bets on them, and at the end of the evening it was agreed that Will had easily won. On the following night he persuaded Lilly to sing with him, and they made a packet!

By this time Steve had dashed out to call Ellen to speak to her daughter. He'd barely left the room when Will, with a somewhat shifty look in his eye, asked,

"Has Dad gone?"

When I told him that he had gone for Ellen, Lilly appeared behind him while, looking decidedly shifty about it, he said to me,

"Mum, what would you say if we told you we want to get married?"

Of course, what he really meant was, 'what would Dad say?', and immediately I knew just what Steve's first question would be!

"Oh Will! Dare I guess why? Didn't Dad warn you about not letting this happen? You know Lilly, I love you like a daughter, but I really thought Will would show more responsibility than that. Goodness knows what your parents will say."

I didn't get chance to say another word as they had just walked in the door behind me.

"What we'd say about what Mel?" Bob asked.

Ellen shot me a quick glance which seemed to show that she had a pretty good idea of just what this revelation was going to be. It took Bob a few seconds longer to catch on, but then Steve came in the room behind him just in time to hear me trying to find a gentle way to put this news from our respective offspring.

Well, the look on his face said it all, though the words from his mouth (at least those fit to repeat) left not a thing to the imagination! He went ballistic, using language I could only assume must have been picked up all those years ago during his military life! Will tried repeatedly to get a word in now and again, but with no luck. Even Lilly attempted to intervene, but Steve would have none of it. He was fuming, and would take no apology from Will, or accept Lilly's word that it had been as much her fault, and one she certainly didn't regret. As she said to the anxious gathering of parents, this was a joint decision to marry; the fact that their celebrations over this decision had been the cause of her condition was as much hers as his!

I hesitated to bring up one 'small' matter which I felt Steve had overlooked. Should I brave it and intervene with my thoughts at this point, or would it have an adverse effect on Steve's conversation with them both? Or come to that, should I even remind Bob and Ellen about a small matter they may never have mentioned to their daughter?

I had no chance to give this more thought as it happened. Steve was just setting off on yet another rant about 'responsibility' and 'respect' for Lilly when it was Will's job to keep her safe when, to my horror, he stepped forward in front of Lilly, thrust out a very determined chin, and tackled his father with the very thought which I'd just been mulling over!

"Now just you hang on a minute Dad; do the words 'pot' and 'kettle' mean anything to you? Do you really reckon my maths skills are so bad that I can't take my date of birth from the date of your wedding and see quite a distinct gap there? I've never seen anyone complain about that, and as long as we stick together because we really want to, why should that matter anymore for us than it did for you two?"

Oh hell, I wondered just what response this would bring! To my surprise though it seemed to pour water on the fire of Steve's wrath, and completely disarm him for a 'very' brief second. What was coming next I had no idea … none of us did, but it did seem that the rest of us were all hanging on Steve's reaction before showing our own. All I could do, out of view of the camera, was to put a hand gently on Steve's arm, and throw him a quick half smile which I hoped showed him that we were in no real position to hold the moral high ground. To my great relief, and I believe that of Bob and Ellen, he threw his son a grin which clearly said, 'Ok, you win', and said,

"Well ok, as long as Lilly's parents are ok with it. But just you remember that even though your maths might be right, we are still, and always will be together, so you've never had to worry about your parents splitting up over all these years like so many do. If this is really what you want it's all or nothing, do you understand me son?"

Will jumped up from the chair he'd been sitting on and, pulling himself up to his full height, did a very passable salute and said,

"Yes Sergeant Lockett, sir."

Chapter Eight

When our wanderers finally returned to the fold they were greeted warmly by all those they had known before they left all those months ago. It did seem that no one else had been particularly surprised about their news. Though I say 'months', to myself and Ellen it felt more like a few years. We were keen to begin making preparations for their wedding, but felt we needed to leave it to them to say just what they wanted, not just to take over like a couple of overbearing mothers.

As so long ago with our wedding, we were still lucky enough to have Josh and Mia there to take on the huge task of catering for all the families and friends for the event. We sat with Will and Lilly for some time attempting to reduce the numbers, but it seemed that as fast as we took one off, we added another two! The actual marriage was to be held in the marquee on the lawn. The spring weather made this possible. In the end it was decided to make it just a buffet in the evening, with the food and drink being laid out in the entrance hall. From there guests could pass in and out of the main hall where there was to be live music. Being an assortment of Grange residents, university pals, and a large contingent from both families, this was no light undertaking, but with all pulling together, we were thrilled with the way it all came together.

Of course, Lilly didn't have to look for her husband to drop from the sky by parachute as I had, Will was already there at the end of the aisle, waiting nervously for her to enter the marquee. When she did she looked absolutely radiant. Ellen had actually made her dress (something I could never do), and Bob walked up the aisle with her on his arm looking the proudest man on earth! It was clear to see the love glow between bride and groom. Unusually, Will had asked his father to be his best man, a thing that thrilled Steve to think Will thought so highly of him to ask. Mind you, I did wonder of the wisdom of this move, knowing Steve would find the most embarrassing stories for his best man's speech, and so it proved to be!

As people started to move through into the main hall I heard the live band Steve had organised strike up. I'd not heard them play before and so was pleasantly surprised to find they sounded good. By this time most of the guests had moved through to listen to them, but under orders from Steve, nobody had yet taken to the dance floor. They waited patiently until a very proud father stepped forward to announce that now the bride and groom would come forward for their first dance. I must admit to being just mildly surprised as I had no idea that either of them (especially Will) could dance, but, reminiscent of our own wedding, there was our son leading his beautiful bride out onto the middle of the room, where they danced to the Ed Sheeran song, 'Thinking out loud.' Just watching them was, to me at least, so hypnotic that for a few seconds I was totally unaware of my dear Steve taking my hand and leading me out to join them, followed by a somewhat reluctant Bob, dragged out by Ellen!

A few moments after this the floor was packed with (mostly younger) friends and family. Our Will had always been a happy chap as he grew up, but this day it was plain to see that he'd never been happier. Steve and I decided to prolong poor Bob's agony and Ellen's amusement by doing a quick change of partners in the midst of the throng, just for one more lap around the floor!

Though my parents were with us that day, they were both in their eighties, and so chose to sit out the dancing with Steve's mother, May. I was pleased to see the newly-weds make a point of sitting with them for some time as, living so far away, they'd not had such a close relationship with Will as they would have liked. Before many minutes Will had them all glued to stories of his and Lilly's foreign travels. Though he'd seen May far more than my parents as she lived that bit closer, he had his father's ways of being able to wrap folk around his little finger, and it was quite entertaining watching from a distance.

Somehow, although we so often held weddings and other functions here at the Grange, there was nothing to beat such a close, family one. Ok, you may say that most of these people are not family, in fact most at some time could have been called 'waifs and strays', drunks or druggies, but those who have been pleased to accept the help we have been offering, and these soon became as one big extended family to us.

The original plan Steve had to offer a place to live and often a chance to get the basics of any of the skills on offer by our older, more experienced residents, most of whom were into their sixties now, was a good one. So many had, over the years, improved their lives, kicked their drink and drug habits, and been helped by Steve to find work or apprenticeships, made possible by his strict regime and no-nonsense attitude, and the fact that Lansdown Grange gave them an address to register.

After the wedding Will and Lilly moved into one of what we called the 'Stable Bungalows'. These had been converted not so long after we moved in. Originally Bob and Ellen and Graham (our carpenter) had been in two of these, but since Lilly was born they had moved into one of the well converted gate houses. We gave Lilly and Will the larger of the two as this was spacious enough for the forthcoming new arrival. In the months following their wedding they had plenty of time to do this up to their own taste. What's more, with Will being so popular with many of our people, there were always plenty of willing hands when the need arose. Needless to say though, the choice of décor was entirely down to the new Mrs Lockett!

I must admit that I'd had my doubts as to whether they would actually want to stay at the Grange once they were married, but Will quickly dispersed any ideas to the contrary, by announcing that, he would not only stay to work with us, but that he was considering investigating part-time courses in counselling. I truly believe this was not just to work with Paul on that side of the business, but because of the knowledge he now had of his father's struggle to recover from his earlier life.

"Where else should we go anyway," he said with one of his father's grins, "You know you'd be lost without me mummy dear; and beside, Dad said I was to find work when I'd got my degree, so I reckon I'd be as much use here as anywhere else! You never know, if I do manage to get qualified as a counsellor, I could be even more use, as well as doing his books."

"Cheeky beggar, don't suppose you've asked him if he wants your help have you?"

"No, but he's not getting any younger you know. And after all, you know he's always been happier doing the more active, organisation stuff around the place, rather than sitting at that desk surrounded by papers."

I had to agree that he was right on that score. Steve was still as much the 'action man' he'd been since we first met, though I couldn't help noticing that he was often beginning to look as if he had the weight of the world on his shoulders. Perhaps Will was right, perhaps it would be good for him to allow someone else to carry some of the weight? If so, there would be no one better to do so than Will, certainly no one else he would even consider trusting to take on such a burden.

I therefore decided to tackle the subject that evening when we were sitting quietly over a glass of wine from a bottle squirrelled away from the wedding stock! Waiting until he was well relaxed with me in my favourite position, snuggled up under his arm on the sofa,

"Have you thought of asking Will to stay on here to work with you, not just to live?"

To my surprise, without hesitation, he took another sip from his glass, looked at me in surprise, and said,

"Well, of course he's going to stay isn't he? I've always assumed he planned on working with me," another sip from his glass then adding, "After all, he'll have to take over the place when I'm past it anyway!"

This was music to my ears; the thought of both my men being here, around me, just where I felt they belonged. Of course, neither had it escaped my notice that Steve was becoming increasingly stressed looking lately, and I knew exactly why that was. The day to day running of Lansdown came easy to him. After all, he had been used to the training and handling of men during his time in the paras, and therefore had no problem gaining the same discipline and respect from the assortment of (mainly) youngsters who arrived here through whatever route, in need of help and a home to get them on their feet again. Ok, we did have the occasional failure, those who thought Steve would be a soft touch and would be a push over, but that concept was soon dashed! In Steve's eyes there was no such thing as a free ride. You either put in the effort to bring about some sort of reform, enough to get you back on track for a proper life with a respectable future, or you're out of here! Once this was made clear to them, the majority set to, worked hard, and appreciated the work Steve put into helping them find work to be able to support themselves independently.

But the main cause of Steve's stress right at that point was the dwindling funds in the bank account, funds we needed to keep the place afloat!

Chapter Nine

Reluctant as he was at first to hand over the reins of finance to Will, Steve soon had to admit to me that this did bring him something of a relief, and chance to concentrate on the more practical aspects of his work. I believe that for a while at least, he could work on the theory that 'what you don't see won't hurt you', but of course that was no long term solution.

Normally we would have avoided saying too much to Will as we knew that he had his mind very much on Lilly and the forthcoming baby, though they still had some months to go, but as it happened there was no need. Just a few weeks into Will being on the task of bookkeeping, it was him who brought up the subject of the financial shortfall. Had he spoken to me about it first I would have suggested a little tact when speaking to Steve, but no … he just blurted it out one morning, just as Steve returned from his group exercise session in the grounds.

"Hey Dad, you never warned me what a mess the finances were in around here…,"

But before he could go on Steve's temper snapped,

"Well, what the hell do you expect me to do about it? I've put in all the cash I had left with the place, and all the money that comes from the charity grant. Now what do you suggest I do?"

Poor Will really wasn't expecting to get his head bitten off like that! For a second he stood speechless, not wanting to make things worse. Then he took the risk of trying to rephrase his earlier words,

"Sorry, I didn't mean it to sound like criticism Dad. What I was meaning was that I'm sure there must be a way round this. Why don't I put my mind to it today while you're over Chris's, then we can put our heads together when we have time during the next few days?"

I took the opportunity to jump in and say what a good idea this sounded to me, before Steve had chance to go back on the defensive again. I knew him well enough to know that one thing that really got his back up was being spoken to like a useless old man! There was certainly nothing useless about my man, and neither was he old. After all, he was still only fifty-four years old, and quite literally, fighting fit, just as much as he'd been since I first met him (and obviously, long before!). As many of the young, supposedly tough guy types, who turned up here thinking it would be like a holiday camp and Steve a push-over, found to their cost that was certainly far from the truth!

After a couple of minutes and a stare at me which clearly said, 'et tu Brute', he heaved a deep and rather tired sigh, and said,

"Ok, degree boy, let's see what our money paid for. I suppose it's possible there might be a solution somewhere, but I'm damned if I can find it."

Just for that brief moment, until he said that, I had almost thought that perhaps he might feel we were ganging up on him, but somehow I knew that he had enough faith in me to know I wouldn't do that.

As the next few weeks went by though, there was a definite change in Steve. At first I couldn't work out exactly what the problem was, until I became aware that he'd taken to having a few more drinks than he'd been in the habit of having ... in fact, quite a few more! At first I said nothing as this didn't seem to affect him until the later afternoon or evening, by which time I tried to find ways to distract him. I even went to the lengths after a while of removing the odd bottle from the cabinet in the hope this would stop him. Needless to say, the only affect this had was to send him into the village to restock! In all our years together I must say that I'd never known him drink so heavily. It was pretty clear he was sinking into depression caused by the realisation that he just might be losing his dream to keep Lansdown going.

Anyway, on one particular day I was glad to see Steve load up the mini-bus with our newest group of scruffy looking youngsters. He had arranged to take this group across to our friend Chris who ran an activity centre some distance away as he did from time to time. There was a good selection of things to challenge them with (including that awful climbing wall!), and, with help from Chris and the staff there, these days always managed to show those with low self-esteem just what they were capable of if they put their minds to it. And of course, at the same time as doing this, it gave Steve and Chris a chance to get together and reminisce on their army days! He always came back feeling so much more relaxed after one of these trips, and anyway, I rang Chris ahead of their arrival, just to have a chat and tell him to see if he could do anything to 'calm the savage beast', as it were! It was getting difficult to know from day to day whether poor Steve was going to be like that, or just the opposite, depressed, and especially since he'd been drinking so regularly. I did explain to Chris about this latest habit Steve was forming and how worried I felt about it.

"Like that is it Mel? I thought last time I saw him he was a bit uptight, but I didn't push it. Don't worry girl, I'll have a word in his shell-like and see if I can sort him out a bit."

For a second or two I thought perhaps I'd done a silly thing. Perhaps, if Steve knew we'd been talking about him behind his back it could make him worse, but Chris quickly picked up on my concerns,

"Don't worry, I promise I won't drop you in it. He knows I know him well enough to pick up on his moods. Leave him to me and I'll see what I can do."

"Thanks Chris, I appreciate that, but please don't let on that we've been talking about him behind his back."

Of course I needn't have worried on that score. If anyone could tackle Steve without getting their head bitten off it was Chris, and he knew him well enough to know he had to use great tact!

While I'd been talking to Chris, Will had popped back to the bungalow to have a belated breakfast with Lilly. When he came back to the office I was taken by surprise by his complete change of mood. Where he'd been a little subdued earlier by his father's rather abrupt attitude, he bounded into the room obviously bursting with some new enthusiasm.

"Do you know what Lilly was watching on TV?"

What a silly question I thought. Of course I didn't, I'd been up here on the phone most of the time. How did he think I'd know that when there wasn't a television in the room?

"Not a clue. Why, should I?"

"Well, she'd just put it on ready to watch some programme about gardening that she tells me is on today, but it was too early."

I could feel myself getting close to telling him to do something more productive than watch television while there's so much to do around here. I was about to put those thoughts into words, when he interrupted my thoughts,

"She was watching that Tony Maningly bloke; you know, the one who does the morning chat show." I must have looked a bit blank in his direction, "I'm sure you'd know who I meant if you saw him Mum."

I must have still looked a bit blank. That didn't stop him though, he just pushed on with,

"Come through here Mum," and disappeared through the door into our sitting room next door.

By the time I'd followed him through he had the TV switched on and signalled for me to sit next to him and watch. I have to admit that I couldn't help feeling I was missing the point here somehow. This chap was interviewing a woman about her growing chain of fashion outlets. Clearly they had met previously as he was asking her about the increase in business since her last appearance. I watched patiently as she paraded one after another of her (too skinny) models across the stage to show off her wares, but at the end of the programme had to admit to Will that I really could see no connection between her and his father! In fact there seemed absolutely no connection that I could see.

Well, I must say that my first reaction was to burst into laughter at the picture in my mind of poor Steve having anything to do with fashion, but the unusually stern look I was getting from my son soon encouraged me to pull myself together and listen to what he'd said.

"No Mum, you're not getting my point. I'm not suggesting Dad puts on a fashion show. What I'm suggesting is that if he was to go on the programme and talk about Lansdown, it could bring it to people's attention, you know, raise its profile, and perhaps bring in a few extra funds."

"But honestly Will, could you really imagine him wanting to go on national television and admit to everyone that he wasn't coping? You know how proud he is, and he'd look on that as admitting defeat wouldn't he? You know as well as I do by now that he's never asked anyone for anything. Everything he has he's worked for and achieved on his own. You ask your Nanny May, she'll tell you that's always been his way."

"I suppose you're right Mum, but perhaps this might be a good time to make an exception to that rule if he wants to keep the place going."

On that note we agreed that, just perhaps, we should try to find some tactful way to suggest Will's idea to him, but seeing the vast improvement in his mood when he returned from Chris, perhaps just not that very day!

Chapter Ten

As it happens we were still mulling over Will's idea the following day. I really didn't want to stir Steve out of the happier, more relaxed state he'd come back in the night before, and Will wasn't sure if he was brave enough to try. I think too that Lilly had given him a few words on the subject of tact and timing. As it happened though, there was very little time that day to sit around chatting, let alone watching a chat show on TV.

Steve had appointments lined up to take two of his 'reformed' youngsters for interviews. One had arrived here after several months on the streets. He had no qualifications, no home, and no prospects, but since his arrival had spent time working alongside Pete, our builder. It seemed that he had found something he really enjoyed, something he felt gave him satisfaction, and Steve had found a firm not too far away who were prepared to take him on as an apprentice.

The second chap had been working in the gardens with Bob and Ellen and there was a fellow not so far away who had a good business, travelling around in his van doing gardens for anyone needing help. He had asked Steve to say if he ever found someone who would be interested in helping him in return for board and lodging. This was just what the other lad had wanted. That would be one less mouth to feed and if the other one worked hard in his apprenticeship, there was every hope of him earning sufficient to find a flat to rent eventually.

Later on, once again we both chickened out of bringing up the subject of Will's big idea. Me because I was still enjoying seeing him feeling more relaxed frame of mind, and Will because ... well, I think because he was just a bit frightened of the response he might get! I suggested we leave it until later, much later as far as I was concerned. Anyway, as Steve was busy that day and Will, Lilly and myself had decided to drive down to pay a visit to May, we decided it was best left until the right moment came to bring it up.

It was good to see May again. I knew that Jamie and Sally were regular visitors in her house, but I always felt so much better when I could check for myself that she was coping. Though she already had two granddaughters, she was always thrilled to see her only grandson. Since he was small she always had a soft spot for him. It was clear right back then that she saw so much of his father in him, and loved nothing more than to sit him on her knee and read to him. He, in turn, would cuddle up to her and take in every word she uttered!

Of course one of her first questions was to ask how the Grange was going along. I had decided not to worry her with the truth, but of course Will was not as circumspect as me! Before I had chance to throw him a warning glance he innocently blurted out about Steve, as he put it, 'getting his knickers in a twist' because he was short of funds!

"Oh dear, is that right Mel? Is it really that bad dear?"

Of course I tried to play it down, but I could see she didn't believe me for a moment. I shot an accusing look at Will, and he jumped in quickly to limit the damage his first remark had done by assuring her that there was really no need to panic though, Steve had put him in charge of finances now,

"So we'll soon get that under control Nan."

Though she gave him a reassuring smile I could see that, underneath this show of grandmotherly faith, she wasn't entirely convinced. She tactfully changed the subject by turning to Lilly to ask after the pregnancy. Lilly was pleased to tell her how well she was keeping, and that the doctors had said that everything was progressing as expected. As she told May,

"I'm really looking forward to the day to bring this one into the world."

May and I exchanged sly glances at one another which both were saying, 'you might not find it as easy as you're thinking when the time comes', both remembering the (certainly in my case) pain that comes with this experience! Lilly was right though to look forward to the birth of their child, mine and Steve's grandchild. How time has flown by since that fateful meeting when he came to my rescue? So much has happened since then.

My reverie was interrupted by May telling Will to go into the dining room and bring the box near the window. He duly did as he'd been told, coming back with a sizeable cardboard box in his arms.

"Whatever have you got in here Nan? Feels like a box of bricks!"

"Well yes, there are some of those in there, but just those toy ones you used to play with when you were a little chap. Do you remember how cross you'd get if you couldn't get them to stack up neatly?"

That was true. Just like his father, he was never happy with second best if he tried stacking bricks but had problems keeping them balanced. The difference was that Steve would persevere with such things where Will would tire of trying and knock them all over the place!

"I think you'll find there's a lot of things in there that you'll recognise from when you were small. I wondered if you and Lilly could take them for your little one. After all, I think I'm a bit too old to play with them myself don't you?"

Whilst the three of them sat rummaging through the box of treasures, I took myself to the kitchen and made lunch for us all. As I was doing this my mobile rang in my pocket. I took it out to find it was Steve ringing me.

"Hi Steve, how are things going for you up there? Have you had any luck with those two lads?"

"Well yes, you could say that. The problem is that while I was in Coventry sorting that fellow with his apprenticeship, I seem to have swapped him for three more!"

I heaved a sigh, thinking to myself would he ever learn to say no!

"Ok, tell me, how did you manage to do that this time? I thought you said we needed to thin out the numbers until we raised the finances a bit. Who asked you to take these three then?"

"Well," he said with a rather sheepish tone to his voice, "Nobody really I suppose. You see, I was just heading back to the car and ... well, they were just sitting in the bus shelter looking all cold and bedraggled. Don't know what it's like there, but it's chucking it down up here; and well ... anyway, I was peckish, so I dashed into a burger place and ..."

"And of course you couldn't help buying four burgers instead of just one eh? I suppose they are genuine, not just scroungers?"

I could see his face in my mind, with those sympathetic, big brown eyes, assuring me that, of course, they did genuinely need our help. Though I know just how gentle and caring he is with those he loves, I do also know that he's by no means a push over for anyone on the make. He has never suffered fools or scroungers lightly, so I knew that it was certain these were genuine cases in need of help.

"Oh ok; so what you're telling me is that we're two down, but one up then?" Trying to disguise the sigh I heaved, all I could say was,

"Ok, I reckon there's room in the dormitories for them. We won't be too late home. Just tell Josh or Mia there's three more mouths to feed, and see they get kitted out with towels and something clean to wear."

"Ok, will do. Give my love to Mum. Tell her I'll come next time. See you later."

I took the lunch in to the others and passed on his message to May, but kept the news of our growth in numbers to myself. Far be it for me to spoil a good day out by causing further worry to anyone. That could wait until tomorrow.

Chapter Eleven

"Hey Dad, did I see a new face in the exercise group this morning?"

Trying not to look too bothered, Steve just nodded at Will and said,

"Well, shows how well you look. There were actually two, and a girl, but she wasn't up to it today"

Will heaved a noticeable sigh and said,

"Oh Dad; I thought we were trying to cut down? You'll have to learn to look the other way sometimes you know."

"Ok for you to say that you know. You've never been in that position have you? You've never had to rough it out in the cold, or rummage in bins for food! One of these days I'll take you out for a spell of that life and see how you cope without your home comforts."

"Perhaps I might take you up on that offer one day. Meanwhile we need to get this place ticking over a bit better first. On that subject I have had an idea we could talk over after breakfast. I'll see you in the office when you're ready and we can talk about it."

Steve threw him a quizzical look and agreed to talk after a shower and breakfast, and I must admit to considering whether or not to join them or 'just happen' to be needed somewhere else. No, I decided that would be a cowardly thing to do, but I still couldn't for one minute see Steve taking to the idea of going on TV. For all he'd achieved over the years, he was still an extremely private person underneath it all. Barely before I'd washed our breakfast things Will was back, and so I had no time to beat a tactical retreat, even if I'd tried! As he came into the office where we were right then, Steve looked up and grinned at him and said,

"Right, come on then, let's hear this big idea of yours then. What have you thought of that we haven't already tried?"

"Publicity Dad, that's what you haven't thought of. I know what you're going to say; you do make it known around the immediate area, but perhaps you need to spread the news a bit further afield."

Steve threw him a bewildered, and somewhat aggravated look,

"So you reckon that, if we're struggling to keep the ones we've got here now, we should advertise for more? You must be mad boy. How do you suggest that'll help might I ask?"

I found myself with the sudden urge to beat a retreat at that point, knowing as I did just what Will was about to say next, and pretty sure I already knew what Steve's reaction to that would be.

"No Dad, that's not what I had in mind. I don't suggest you advertise. What I do suggest is that we think of a way to publicise the good work we do here and hope that brings in enough interest to encourage a bit of sponsorship or ..."

"Or charity I suppose you're going to say. Well if you think I'm going cap in hand to the public for hand-outs, you can think again!"

Will heaved a sigh and looked at me, obviously appealing for me to back him up. Having given his idea a little thought the previous day I must say I was coming round to it, but how to bring Steve round was quite another matter. For all he had put into his work here to help those in need of it, he wasn't one to go around shouting about it and certainly wouldn't be keen to do so now. After all, he had spent a good two years hiding away from the world by blending into the background, yet during this time he had, in his own way, often found ways to help others in need.

"Well Steve," I timidly dared interject, "I suppose we should remember that a good chunk of the money we used to start up in the first place did come from charity. Besides, if people heard about your work here and felt it was something worthwhile, would it really be charity in the true sense of the word? It could be looked on as their way of easing their own conscience perhaps?"

For a minute he just stood looking from me to Will and back, clearly thinking that we were ganging up on him again! Without another word Steve turned away from us and stormed off in a rage, taking poor Will quite by surprise.

About an hour later Will came across his father sitting in the barn with a bottle of whisky, half empty, in his hand!

"What are you doing Dad? Is this your solution to your problems, because if it is it's not going to help you know?"

"No, perhaps not, but it numbs the pain for a while kid. That's all I can do now. Face facts, we'll be finished by the end of the year."

About then I came in behind Will. He looked round at me in despair,

"How long has he been using a bottle to hide behind Mum?"

All I could do was throw him a look which clearly said, 'too long'.

"Well Dad, you won't find the solution at the bottom of that bottle. Perhaps you might find it if you'd forget your bloody pride and listened to my idea in the first place."

"You know Steve, it wouldn't hurt to at least listen to what Will is suggesting you know."

"Ok, hit me with it. What exactly are you suggesting?"

A quick glance of 'thanks' to me from Will, and then he plunged straight in (reminiscent of a man plunging into a tank of sharks!). As he'd done the previous day with me, he ushered Steve up to our rooms and switched on the TV. Once again, there was the same chat show with the host, Tony Maningly, interviewing some comedian I had to admit to not knowing. It appeared he was opening a school for budding comics! Of course Steve was quick to get up off the chair he'd been sat on but, as he'd done with me, Will was quick to stop him and insist he stay there and listen for a minute. Having given him chance to see what the programme was about, Will turned the sound right down, turned to Steve and said,

"You see what I mean Dad? That chap is being interviewed and being seen on national TV. The idea is quite clearly in the hope of raising awareness of his new venture. He's bound to get people wanting to invest in it. People who would otherwise never hear about it if he didn't go on TV."

Light dawned across Steve's face.

"Oh no! What you're suggesting is for me to go on there in front of thousands? You are kidding surely? You don't really see me doing that do you?"

I have to admit to feeling sorry for my poor Steve just then. He looked more scared than I'd ever seen him through all our hard, sometimes (for me anyway) terrifying times since we met! But Will was not hearing a word of argument against his idea. He just pushed on and on, stressing the benefits that could come from Steve telling the nation just why the work we do at Lansdown was so necessary, why it cost so much to keep going, and how we wouldn't be able to do so much longer without occasional outside support.

"Ok, ok ... so why don't you do it then? After all, you wanted to take on the business side of things. You'd be far better at it than me lad. Perhaps you could both do it together?"

He threw an appealing look in my direction, one that clearly said, 'help'. I couldn't help thinking that this was a first. I couldn't ever remember him asking for my help before ... it had always been the other way round! He had a bit of a 'rabbit in the headlights' expression for the briefest of seconds. I had to resist the urge to throw my arms around him on the spot!

Of course, poor Steve had no way out. He had no intention of admitting to being scared and, in spite of what he'd said, he knew that, if anyone should do this, it would have to be him. Somehow I couldn't help thinking that this was possibly the first time he'd allowed himself to be pushed into a corner in his life. He'd always been the one in charge, the one everyone looked to for help, but this whole idea was so clearly well out of his comfort zone.

Even so, with a fair bit of persuasion and encouragement from us both, he did eventually agree to the suggestion that Will (as 'business manager') should enquire about the possibility of the makers of the programme being interested in his idea. To our surprise, within two days, they rang him back showing a keen interest. Steve and I had been out dropping off a mini-bus full of our people at various places of work that morning. Barely before we walked in the door we were met by an excited son,

"Guess what? They've rung to see if Dad's available to go on telly next Tuesday. Apparently the person who was has dropped out, and the producers are keen to get you on Dad. It seems this Tony Maningly bloke is quite intrigued as to what you do here."

I wish I could say that poor Steve was equally as keen, but having agreed to it he knew he was too late to back out now! Though I suppose we had expected it, coming as soon as it did came completely out of the blue, it wasn't at all well received by Steve! Right from the start he'd said he thought this could be a bad idea.

"You know what these programmes are like," he argued, "if they can find fault with what someone does they'll blow it up and make it look worse than it is."

"Well, I suppose they do sometimes, but surely they can't find fault with what we do here can they? After all, what we are offering here is an important service, something unique to Lansdown Grange." Will argued.

Well, I did manage to talk him round on the grounds of encouraging others to follow our example, but I was soon to learn just how naive I was!

Chapter Twelve

We turned up at the studios in plenty of time, but I could soon tell Steve was uneasy with what he called the 'faffing around' we had to put up with. The idea of having to sit there letting the girls see to make-up and hair most certainly didn't exactly fit in with my tough, rugged looking husband! As he said to me, he most certainly wouldn't have let me talk him into it if he'd known they'd be more interested in his appearance than in what he'd achieved back at the Grange.

By the time we actually found ourselves being called to walk onto the set and shake hands with the host, I could tell Steve was already wishing he'd put his foot down about coming. Ok, we were both greeted politely enough by our host, Tony Maningly, but right from the start it was clear that Steve was just not comfortable with any of it.

We were directed to a small sofa opposite Tony, and tried hard (or at least I did) to look at ease with the cameras in our faces, while he gave a short introduction about who we were, and where we'd come from.

I was somewhat relieved that he didn't say a word about Steve's past life in the army, as I knew this was too personal, and anyway, had no bearing on our work at Lansdown. Having done this he then turned to us, Steve in particular, and said,

"I believe you inherited the place where you've set up your business, is that correct Mr Lockett, or may I call you Steve?"

Trying to be patient, Steve grinned at him and said,

"You can call me anything you like as long as it's not rude. So am I ok to call you Tony?"

I could sense the hidden sarcasm in his voice as he said this. I gave him a surreptitious nudge and a half frown when the cameras went off him briefly. He threw back a sneaky grin before they came back to us.

"And you Mrs Lockett," I interrupted him to suggest 'Mel', "I gather you married Steve a few months after moving in there, is that right?"

"Yes, that's right. We had been together for some time before moving in there."

"Do you mind me asking where you met one another?"

I could feel tension rising in Steve!

"We met in Chesterfield. I was in need of help and Steve stepped up to give some."

'Give me some', oh hell … I worded that all wrong! I could see how it could be misinterpreted but I only meant 'to give me the help I needed'! Why do I always put my foot in it? I glanced sideways at Steve, and for a second wondered if he was about to explode with laughter or temper. In the end he managed to supress whichever it was. Somehow we managed to steer the conversation away from the army except a very brief mention of that being his former career. I knew he wouldn't allow the conversation to delve deeper into that, so found myself turning it back to our work at the Grange.

"Since we arrived at the Grange we've been working flat out to bring it round."

"Now Steve, can you explain just how you came to inherit Lansdown Grange please?"

As he did so we could see pictures of the place, both before and after we bought it round to its present condition.

"If you don't mind me saying, that's a damn stupid question. Obviously it was left to me in my Grandmothers will."

"So now, looking at the state of the place when that happened, just how did you find the money to bring it round to what it is now?"

Steve threw him a dirty look … I could feel the temperature rising!

"Not that it's any of your business, but there was a good chunk left me with the place, and we managed to get at a sizeable grant."

Tony tried to calm things briefly by looking in my direction and asking,

"And you have a son I believe? How old is he?"

"Yes, we have just one son, William. Since achieving his business degree he is now working with us as business manager, but also doing a part-time counselling course at Coventry University.

"So, is he like his father, would you say?"

Oh dear. I felt this was going from bad to worse. I caught a glimpse of Steve's face out of the corner of my eye at that point.

"Well, in most ways, yes. Just a younger version, and still in need of more life experience, as most lads his age are. But like his father, he'd do anything for anyone in need of help."

I'd hoped that last remark might steer the conversation back to the subject we'd come for … to appeal to others to do what we were doing and help the less fortunate. Somehow it didn't hit the mark. Tony was determined to show Steve up as a rich fool with nothing better to spend his money on. He couldn't have been further from the truth. In fact we had hoped this might have the effect of helping to raise, not only more funds to help us out, but awareness of the problems of homelessness across the country!

Unfortunately this had just the opposite effect! It seemed to give Tony the opening he was looking for to turn the table on Steve, clearly in the hope of making him look stupid. Big mistake.

"So Steve, one day you'll pass the place on to your son? And what will he do with it when it's his turn? Surely he won't take a beautiful, historic house like Lansdown Grange and fill it with the dregs of society?"

Steve stood up and glared at him,

"And just what do you mean by the 'dregs of society'?"

Obviously thinking that he was on the verge of pushing Steve into admitting to being the fool he thought he was, he went what I knew was just that step too far!

"Well, what would you call the drunks and druggies you take in off the streets who just want to pray off society?"

The grin on his face was enough for me to want to punch him in the mouth, let alone Steve! Now I knew we were in trouble. The cameras were homing in on a fuming Steve as he stepped up to Tony, grabbed him by the lapels on his jacket, pulled him to his feet and bellowed in his face,

"I'll give you 'pray off society'! Have you ever had a day's hardship in your bloody cushy little life you worm! When did you last sleep rough, or have to rummage for food out of bins? When did you ever lose your job and find yourself out on the streets because you couldn't pay your rent. And then how the hell do you reckon they find work if they don't have an address?"

Oh God! All hell was breaking loose. The security men had rushed in to his rescue, but two of them (big ones at that) were no match for Steve. He just stood holding Tony and staring at him as if he wanted to punch him and throw him across the studio.

This was a disaster. Though I agreed with everything Steve said and did, right now I was also aware that half the country was watching. If it got any worse they could well have him arrested! I had to intervene. I went across and put my hand on his arm, and as he glanced down at me I said quietly,

"Come on Steve; it's obvious this fool has never had the experience of living that way, so he's not worth the bother. Let him crawl back under his cosy little rock!"

One final glare of hatred and Steve let go of him and started to walk away with me. But then he stopped ... I wondered what was going to happen next. We were just about to leave the set when he turned, walked back half way toward Tony, and said,

"If you think it's such a joke mate, you come and spend a couple of weeks living rough amongst these 'dregs' with me. I'll show you why we're trying to help them."

For a second or two there was deadly silence all around the studio. Tony tried to give us a sickly smile as if saying that he knew this was a joke, but Steve's expression never changed,

"I didn't think you would. That's the trouble with society these days ... those who have don't give a damn about those who have not, as long as they don't have to mix with them!"

And so saying we left.

The drive back home that day began in complete silence. Steve was clearly too angry to hold any normal conversation, and I didn't know if I dared! After all, although this had been Will's idea, I had gone along with it thinking it would be a good one. He never really wanted to do it at all.

We'd not gone far out of town when we spotted a cafe coming up on our side of the road, and I suggested we stop for a drink before going on. Steve agreed, even agreeing that I drove from then on, a suggestion I made as his driving was somewhat erratic until then. We parked up and went in. I ordered the coffee and waited for it to be poured while Steve found us a table in the corner. All was fine until the woman put the cups on the counter and went to take my cash. As she did so she looked across and saw Steve sitting in the corner.

"Oh my," she said, "That's not the chap from off the breakfast TV is it?"

My heart sank. I wondered what was going through her mind. Should we leave before we stirred up any trouble? Even so, I had to say that yes, it was him. I waited for her reaction.

"Please, put your money away dear," she said, "he was brilliant! Do you think he'd mind if I came over and shook his hand?"

This most certainly took me by surprise. After the way he'd behaved on TV, I genuinely thought he'd blown it now! I certainly didn't expect him to turn into a celebrity. Neither did I know what he would make of this new status. Anyway, I took the chance of taking her across with me and, rather gingerly, telling him she had seen him on TV, and thought he was 'brilliant'. I think he was as surprised as I had been with this reaction to his flare up!

"Do you know Mr Lockett, I've always wanted to give that man a piece of my mind for being so rude to everyone he interviews. I take it he didn't take you up on your offer to go out on the streets? Would you really do that?"

This brought a wide grin to Steve's face.

"Yes, of course I would. I meant every word I said. Perhaps I was a bit out of control, but folk like him really bug me. After all, you shouldn't criticise what you know nothing about. But it was worth calling his bluff. He'd never survive out on the streets on his own. At least I was offering to go with him and show him what to do."

We sat chatting to her while we drunk the coffee, during which time a couple of men on their way to work, and a small group of women on their way back from the school run had come in. Our host took great pride in introducing Steve to them (in spite of his obvious embarrassment), and much to my relief, they queued up to shake his hand and say how he'd got their day off to an exciting start! Mind you, the mums did say that they had to send their kids to play in their bedrooms towards the end as they didn't think the language was entirely suitable for them to listen to.

As you can imagine, when we arrived back home to the Grange we found Bob, Pete and Dave outside the gate, struggling to clear the entrance for us to drive in past the small but growing bunch of press waiting for us to return! Somehow though we did get in, and drove up to the door to a wild reception of cheers and claps from our 'dregs', or residents as we prefer to call them.

For the rest of the week we hardly dare show our faces outside the place. There was a constant stream of press and goodness knows who, ready to pounce if we dare go anywhere near the gate. In fact it didn't stop there. They were getting to be like a swarm of ants, creeping into any crevice they found. Bob found a couple sneaking through his rows of runner beans one morning, hoping to find a way in that way. Needless to say, when he found them he saw to it that they ran faster than the beans!

Josh went into the village for a few supplies one day and found himself hi-jacked by a group of them. Remembering Steve's instructions that we all needed to be careful as to the way we showed ourselves off to these people, he avoided them very cleverly by saying that he must first go in the butchers before talking to them, and then (with the help of the butcher), sneaking out the back door and coming home a different way! I couldn't help thinking what a shame it was that Steve hadn't followed his own suggestion to be careful how he showed himself off to them that day!

On top of all this it proved almost impossible to switch on the TV or open a newspaper without seeing a picture of Steve, holding Tony (almost suspended from the ground!), with all and sundry commenting on that interview.

Meanwhile, when Will was at Uni one day, we had a phone call from him. It seemed that, once news got around that he was Steve's son, he was getting his leg pulled left, right and centre! As it happened, most of this was done in good humour, particularly from a good number of them who clearly wished they had a father like Steve.

Unfortunately there was a small group at the university who decided that what I'd said made him sound a bit like a 'Daddy's boy'. As a consequence, this group cornered him in the quadrangle one afternoon on his way back to his class, obviously intent on roughing him up!

Well, clearly this was a non-starter. It seemed that three of them came at him, one armed with a spade left in the border by the gardener. The first two were quickly dealt with when they found it almost impossible to get near enough to touch him, but the one with the spade was so certain he could finish the job!

It came as something of a shock to the poor lad to find Will grab the spade handle in both hands, roll backwards, and send the poor lad flying over the top and skidding across the lawn, landing on his back with one foot each side of the vice-chancellor's legs!

When Will rang me to tell me what had happened, I must admit to being more than a little anxious. It would be an awful shame if all his hard study was wasted. I was hoping he wouldn't get kicked off the course for fighting, but I gather it was the other lad who got in trouble over this as there was clearly a suitable witness. Even Steve agreed that this was not a case of Will using his skill to fight, it was just used in self-defence, and that was ok.

I was pleased to hear that this event, added to the apparent growing list of admirers Steve seemed to have, had actually served to make Will one of the most popular students on his course! Having kept pretty much to himself until then, apparently he now had something of a following. It pleased his father to hear this, but I decided, as much for the sake of

Lilly as Steve, to keep it to myself when Will told me that all the girls wanted him to ask his father for his autograph!!

All this commotion had now been going on for almost three weeks since that awful day at the TV studio. The two of us had kept out of the limelight since then, worried by the possibility of having undone any good we'd hoped to do. But it seemed that the public and the press were pretty well on our side. This seemed to have been picked up by the programme makers, and of course to Tony Maningly himself. He'd begun to see that his attitude was having a detrimental effect on his reputation. There was even talk in the wings of having him replaced. In the end he could see only one way out of this ... take up that 'idiots' offer of going on the streets with him for a couple of weeks. After all, what harm could he come to? It would give him chance to prove he was right, and that it was possible to live rough for a while without turning to drink, drugs and the filthy state these people live in!

The next morning found him sitting back in the studio, admittedly with a wider gap between the chairs, and with the security men closer to hand, facing a reluctant and belligerent looking Steve (with me back by the security chaps, just as a precaution!).

After a forced smile and greeting, he turned to the camera and put his explanation,

"It seems that on my last meeting with Steven Lockett, much of what I said was perhaps misunderstood by my audience on this show. I have brought Mr Lockett back so that I can make amends and correct the misunderstanding."

He turned and, rather sheepishly, faced Steve with that silly smirk on his face. I watched Steve's face for signs of any reaction; there was none!

"I believe you challenged me to accompany you for a period of living rough, is that right?"

"Yes," was all Steve said, still his face was expressionless.

Obviously feeling a little intimidated by this, Tony continued,

"Ok, Steve, having had time to organise time off from my work, I am now free to take you up on your challenge. Perhaps having a camera filming as we go will allow the audience to see just what you have in mind and …"

"Oh no! No television cameras or the deals off. This is not a publicity stunt. We do it my way or not at all. You can talk about it afterwards, but it's the genuine experience or none."

After Tony had sat in obvious confusion for a brief second or two, no doubt trying to figure how this would work, or how to back out, Steve looked him straight in the eye and said,

"Well? Do we have a deal or not? I say what you're allowed to bring, choose where we go and what we do. You either go along with it to the letter or it's off."

What could the poor fool do but agree, stuck as he was with cameras in his face and Steve's somewhat threatening glare opposite him?

"Ok Steve, I'll do it."

Chapter Thirteen

All of a sudden, instead of feeling we needed to hide away for disgracing ourselves, so much of the country was awash with news of this latest development. All those students at Coventry, especially the girls, were even more full of what was going to happen, making Will even more popular, perhaps a little too much so for Lilly perhaps! Steve insisted that Tony stayed clear of TV and press coverage, and that he remained indoors for the two weeks leading up to the time he'd chosen to leave. In fact, although I knew, he refused to tell another soul just when that would be. He told him he wasn't to shave for that couple of weeks. I gather that didn't go down well, and so, for the second week Steve invited himself to move in with Tony to keep a check of what he was doing!

By the time it came to the day I knew they were to embark on their adventure, Steve had made certain they were both looking suitably scruffy in appearance. For my part, I had done as he asked and contacted his mate Chris (also an ex-para), to come to a pre-arranged point during the night to pick the two of them up. As Steve told me, going after dark and over the garden wall away from prying eyes would mean there was less chance of the press following them. The plan was for Chris to take them, with Tony blindfolded, to an unknown destination to start their journey.

I dearly wished I could have gone with them to see just how they coped. I knew of course that Steve could cope with no problem; after all, that was how he was living when we first met. And even then he did have the advantage of his army training behind him which taught self-sufficiency, but I doubted Tony had ever had a day of hardship in his life. I could picture Steve wearing pretty much the same old worn out stuff he'd been wearing back when I met him, and by now allowed his beard to grow enough to serve as a disguise to those not too familiar with him.

Even so, though I had no doubt I knew just what he'd look like, even I had not a clue as to where Chris had dropped them off. All I could be sure of was that by now Tony must be somewhat shaken, having been dragged from his bed in the middle of the night and practically taken prisoner by some unknown figures, thrown in the back of an old van blindfolded. Once they released him and left him alone with Steve it would have left him pretty shaken! That would have been a few hours ago now and I could imagine that by this time he would be wondering where breakfast was coming from ... and I also knew Steve would be beginning his education in the way to find food without cash just as he had me that first year.

I thought back to the ways he could always find to see we didn't go too hungry. Obviously we could always have eaten more than we had, but neither did we starve. I wondered if they'd find a friendly old chap like the one who let Steve bed down in his allotment shed, in return for some digging. Often that provided us with a couple of potatoes which could be wrapped in foil and baked in the hot embers of the old chap's bonfire! Coincidentally, it was yet another allotment owner whose hens provided us with eggs for our breakfast. The big difference here being that this one had no clue about this! As Steve said, they laid far too many for him to miss a couple!

I remembered the cheek of my man when he actually sneaked into a barn one day and milked one of the cows before the farmer came to do it. And then he'd roared with laughter when I was surprised to find it was warm. I still giggle when I remember him telling me that you don't get refrigerated cows!

During the course of the first couple of days they were gone, I had occasion to go looking for Dave as I had a minor problem with a blocked pipe. When I couldn't find him anywhere I questioned Pete as to his whereabouts, and he (reluctantly) let me into a secret I'd not been privy to. It seemed that Steve had recruited a number of our chaps from the Grange to act different parts, either as smart business men, or in some cases, as real rough characters (some of these were those recently reformed from just that type).These were then sent out to meet up 'by chance' as it were, to see to it that Tony got the full experience during their time, and most of these were also equipped with hidden cameras, supplied by Chris, so that Steve had a record of events which Tony could not dispute. Apparently the plan was to have the TV and press meet them back here at Lansdown on their return, and Steve wanted them to get a true picture, rather than a yarn spun by Tony to defend his reputation.

As you can imagine, every time I poked my nose outside the gate I found myself surrounded by press, wanting to know just where Steve had gone with Tony, and why they were not allowed to follow them! By the end of the first couple of days I began to get pretty annoyed with this, but not so much as when I heard from Steve's brother, Jamie, that he'd called round to see his mother one evening, and had to fight his way past another group of them gathered outside her house and pouncing on her at every possible opportunity. I was fuming; poor May could have done without that, so I rang her and suggested she pack some things and I would get Will to pick her up and come here until this was all over. She was more than glad to do so, and I knew Will wouldn't let these people get in his way.

Once here, most evenings, Lilly and Will would come up, and the four of us would sit together in the evenings watching the constant speculation on the TV as to the complete disappearance of one of their chief personalities! Though I could quite honestly say that I had no more answer than them as to where he'd be, I did have a pretty good picture in my mind of just how they'd be living.

That much I had in common with practically all the residents, past or present, with them all having found themselves in just that position through no fault of their own. I think the majority of them were under the illusion that Steve wouldn't make it quite as bad as they had coped with though, but I soon put them straight on that score.

"You've surely all got to know him well enough by now to know he never does anything by halves. He promised the fool the full experience, but I bet he too had imagined it would be a watered down version, but that's just not Steve. It would be defeating the object."

I couldn't help feeling just a tiny bit sorry for the poor chap, but amused at the same time, but then he had agreed to do this after all. And if his experience had the desired effect on just one person it would be worth whatever Steve was putting him through.

None the less, I must admit to feeling better knowing we had May safely tucked up under our roof. We had been aware over the past year of her becoming quite a bit frailer. Knowing she had twenty-four hour company, and was surrounded by so many folk she now thought of as friends, gave her a feeling of added security. I soon noticed a vast change in her, for the better I might say, and made a suggestion to young Will one day.

"I was wondering, now you and Lilly are in the bungalow, would you have any objections to May staying in your old room here permanently? I think it would be good for her to have us all around her now."

He looked at me in what I thought was a look of bewilderment, but then said,

"What a daft question Mum. You must know I wouldn't mind. It would be good to have her here. She shouldn't be that far away and on her own anyway. And besides, if I'm not using the room there's no reason to leave it empty. Anyway, if you have her to fuss over perhaps you won't be fussing round me so much ... I have got Lilly to do that now after all!"

And so, with May jumping at the chance to come here to be near Steve, that was settled before he came home! We spent the next day emptying out the last of Will's belongings which were still tucked away in odd corners, and converted it into a very comfortable Granny flat!

Chapter Fourteen

While Steve was gone we moved the rest of Will's things across into what was, after all, now his home in the bungalow, and then taking her followed by a large convoy of press, back to her home in Cambridgeshire to sort what to bring with her, and what to leave. Jamie and Sally set to with Will and myself to pack everything she wanted into the van we'd borrowed for the day. As for the furniture, she only chose to bring a few of her favourite pieces at that time as it had been decided that Jamie and Sally should move out of their rented Cambridge flat and into May's house.

It felt good having her here where we could keep her safe and give her the company she was beginning to miss now that all her family had 'flown the nest'. Although Sally and Jamie were not far from her, and I gather were always glad to visit for a good home cooked meal, at the end of the day she was still very much alone in a house which had, for so long, been bustling with activity and chatter.

I must say that I was glad of some female company while Steve was away. Though there was Ellen and two or three other younger girls at the Grange, somehow it felt good to settle down in the evenings and speculate as to where he had taken poor Tony. Of course, May had never had the first-hand experience I had had that first year, and though at first she found it hard to believe her son had lived that way, in the end I believe she got as much amusement as me from just imagining what the poor chap must be going through! In fact, we would amuse ourselves in the evening by watching the news, any news from any part of the country, to see if we could catch a glimpse of Steve in disguise, lurking about or just passing by in the background of any news report across the country. Of course we never did.

There was just once when I caught a fleeting glimpse of a slightly familiar face in the background of one report about traffic congestion in London, but if it was him, he was huddled up under a dirty looking hoody, outside a branch of a burger bar. I didn't get chance to see if he was alone as a bus passed by just then, but as this went by, and just as the camera was moving away from there, I'm sure a scuffle broke out in the doorway and the man in the hoody appeared to step in! Could this have been Steve I wondered?

At first when I said this to May, she was a little shocked. She was concerned that he could have been hurt. But I believe even she could see why I didn't seem worried about this after I told her how efficiently he'd dealt with the druggies back at Chesterfield, leaving all three knocked out and deposited in a large shop skip! She was now beginning to form a whole new picture of her eldest son, and could understand too just why I loved him as I do, even after having witnessed his massive breakdown at the finale of our first year together.

One evening, a couple of days before he was due home, we were sitting quietly together, watching some rubbish programme on TV, when May looked round at me with a slightly worried expression on her face and said quietly,

"You know Mel, I'm so glad Steve has you. I can see from what I know of him, and what you've told me, that he needs you as much as you tell me that you need him."

She hesitated before going on, and then, taking my hand in hers, she continued,

"You won't ever leave him dear will you, I mean … you'll look after him for me when I'm gone, won't you?"

I was shocked by the sincerity in her voice. For a brief second I was lost for words.

"May, why are you even asking that? You must know I couldn't survive without him, and anyway, what do you mean 'when you're gone'? What a thing to say. You've got many years ahead of you yet, and you're going to spend them here with us, where you can look after him with me. Let's face it, he's handful enough to need two women to keep him in order after all."

This last comment did bring a smile to her face and a little laughter to her voice, but even so I couldn't help wondering what had brought on this sudden concern on her part. But then, I suppose, she had never completely recovered from that awful period in her life when she felt he was lost to her forever. I made a mental note to talk this over with Steve when he returned, but meanwhile did my best to make light of such things by telling her some of the more comical thing that he had put me through during that first year!

She did seem much comforted by the idea that, by those months of dragging me around the country to evade both the police and Jake's murderer, he had proved to be still the strong, capable son she knew him to be, not quite the wreck she had been worrying about for so long.

It was also really pleasing to see the close attachment she was building with young Will. Though perhaps I shouldn't say it, though I knew how much she loved Tom's two daughters, I could tell she had a particularly soft spot in her heart for him. This could have been because he was her only grandson, but I can't help thinking it was more to do with him being the son of Steve, her first-born.

One evening when Will and Lilly were sitting with us (also glued to the news on the hope of catching a glimpse of Steve!), I overheard him asking about Steve's father, his grandfather. I immediately felt a shiver run down my spine, thinking how she would take this question, in light of the fact that Peter had actually been Steve's step-father. I wished I had known this was going to be something he'd ask, as I doubted she'd want to admit to having been raped. I wanted to change the subject, in fact I tried, but before I could do so May shook her head at me and said,

"No dear, the lad is old enough to know the truth. I owe him that much, and I owe it to his father not to leave it to him to explain."

Beckoning a bewildered looking Will to sit alongside her on the sofa, May took hold of his hand in hers and began her story. It seemed from the way she did so that she had at last, with much support and reassurance from Steve, felt able to brush away any remaining traces of shame attached to the affair. Now, to her mind, she had allowed her love of Peter Lockett, and of the son he had been proud to adopt as his own, to brush away any trace of shame, and no longer felt the need to hide this from the world.

She explained to him about his great-grandparents having been employed at Lansdown Grange as gardener and housekeeper, and (with just the smallest of shivers running through her) that it had been their son, Henry, who had actually been the one who had raped her.

"Oh, so this Henry bloke was actually my grandfather then? Guess he's long gone? If he wasn't by now he would be if I caught up with him!"

"Will!" I interjected, "that's not very nice now, is it?"

As he looked in my direction I couldn't help catching a clear glimpse of his father's temper flash across his face.

"Neither was what he did to Nan, was it?"

But he said no more on that subject, realising that it would possibly upset May. His next question took me totally by surprise.

"Anyway, I wish I'd know Peter Lockett. He must have been a very special man. Do you mind Nan if I ask where is he buried?"

"Of course not dear. His ashes are buried in the churchyard by the little church on the hill. The same place as your great-grandparents. Perhaps we could go up there sometime? I would love to visit him. He would have been so proud to see what your father has done here, and what an amazing family you all are."

The genuine warmth of the hug he gave her as he got up to go out left me feeling so proud of our boy. It was so rewarding to see just what a kind, sensitive young man he had grown into, and just how much of his father there was in him. Perhaps he'd never be quite as tough and capable physically, but in appearance, and in the sensitivity and thoughtfulness he showed to those he cared for, there was nothing to choose between them. And now, in just a few months, he and Lilly would be proud parents of yet another generation of

Lockett's! I wonder ... would this be yet another boy, or would we be greeting a new girl into the family? That was still unknown to us as Lilly and Will had decided to keep that piece of secret information to themselves, leaving it as a surprise to us all a little longer before telling us! Either way, we would all be more than happy to welcome this little one to our number.

"Anyway Will," I said, catching a glimpse of Lily out of my eye, "I think that can wait until tomorrow. Poor Lilly here is nearly asleep. You're ready for your bed tonight I think young lady, aren't you?"

I could see her eyes were gradually drooping, but as I said this she looked up with an embarrassed expression on her face,

"Oh sorry. I didn't mean to be rude. But you're right Mrs Lockett, I am pretty shattered. Do you mind?"

"Of course not dear; but there is one thing I do mind," she threw a worried glance in my direction, "Will you stop calling me 'Mrs Lockett'! After all these years you should be used to calling me Mel, ok?"

She threw me a warm smile, gave both me and May a gentle hug, and allowed herself to be led off to their bungalow for an early night.

Chapter Fifteen

The following morning we all had to pull together once more to fulfil, not just our usual roles around the place, but those which were always Steve's particular ones. Happy as I was to help out with the exercise sessions, I did decide that Will was best placed to take those who were up to it for the regular jog, on this occasion around the grounds. Usually Steve would set off out through the gates, often heading off around the lake or through the woods, but the seemingly permanent gathering of press still crowding around made it easier to stay closer to home. I was pleased that Steve had spent so much time with me over the years, teaching me self-defence which I was able to pass on now to a growing group of young women (on condition this was strictly to be used combined with self-control), plus I also had acquired a good knowledge of yoga, and so this was my first job of the day. By the time we'd finished these duties, showered, and eaten breakfast, I left Lilly and May in our sitting room (once again glued to news from around the country ('just in case'), while Will stepped up to sort the morning post and other necessary paperwork. I was so genuinely pleased to hand over that particular responsibility to him, but then he did want to step up as business manager, and while Steve was away was a good opportunity to prove himself.

Meanwhile I did my usual walk about, my chance to see everyone was happy, that there was no serious unrest in the camp! As I found most of the residents still sitting around in the hall staring at the (rather large!) television there, it seemed the whole place was on 'Steve watch'! Every now and again someone would point to the screen and say they thought they'd seen him, but inevitably they were wrong.

"Go on Mel," someone begged, "Tell us where he's gone?"

Of course I couldn't. Josh laughed from the kitchen doorway,

"He wouldn't have told her anyway. He knows women can't keep secrets."

I threw him a dirty look, but had to agree with him to the point that he wouldn't, and certainly did not, tell anyone.

"Anyway, if you lot have nothing better to do you could check your rooms and dorms are tidy. I shall be coming round soon for your weekly inspection. And don't think just because Steve's not here you can live like pigs! You all need to keep your standards up if you ever expect to build better lives."

Well, I don't think I gave a very good impersonation of my husband, but just the fact that they knew what he'd say if they didn't listen to me sent them all scuttling off to prepare for a 'Sgt Lockett' style inspection!

It was always gratifying to see those, especially youngsters who came into us after spending time on the streets through whatever reason, gradually change from dirty, scruffy, sometimes drug or drink addicts, into rehabilitated and presentable people with a sense of pride in their appearance and a willingness to take a full and active part in society once more. Though there were always those we were unable to help, those who thought this was an easy way to get someone else to provide for them, on the whole the majority took Steve's rules seriously, and accepted this as chance to get clean, perhaps try out a basic trade of some sort or, when they were ready, to accept help finding work to support themselves in the outside world.

One thing we noticed over the years has been an increase in the number of ex-forces people who seem to have found their way to our gates. Since Steve's time in the army it has become apparent that those coming out of the military suffering with PTSD have felt a little more at ease talking about their problems to him, and in particular Paul, about how this affects them. We felt that these were amongst the most rewarding of our achievements. After all, it had been Paul's skill as a trained counsellor that had managed to straighten out Steve so long ago after his breakdown. Amongst the number of these we found the need to expand some of our accommodation to allow for the odd married couple, especially in the case of some who had previously lived in married quarters. Some were quite short term until they found homes in the area which allowed them to continue to come in for Paul's sessions, or just to feel a part of semi-military life as it were, in the form of the more light-hearted gatherings Steve loved to arrange regularly. Needless to say, the majority of our youngsters (non-military) were not encouraged to join these!

Even so, this need to keep expanding the accommodation on the estate was one of the main causes of the dwindling of our coffers. The people in the local area had been brilliant. So often we had found that someone, somewhere was running an event of some sort, and more often than not we would find that they would donate a good portion, if not all, of the proceeds to Lansdown Grange. It was so satisfying to find just how much they had taken us to their hearts and made an effort to see the benefits of such a place.

Of course, during the time Steve was away, we still had the odd events to cater for. There were two weddings, both of which had been planned to take place in the large marque outside, but on both occasions the weather threatened to spoil them, and so we took the decision to change them to the main hall. As it turned out, the first of these did turn out to be a far better day than had been forecast, but this didn't seem to worry the couple involved, so we felt that we were justified in this. On the other hand, the day of the second one turned out to be torrential rain and howling wind all day. Though that wedding party were not happy when they arrived to find we were ushering them inside, hardly before they'd stepped out of the cars the rain and wind hit them and sent them running for cover!

Josh and Mia did a brilliant job catering for such events. Of course, over the years since working together, Mia had gone from the lost, lonely street girl, to a confident and capable chef, thanks to the help from Josh. Between them they, in turn, had brought on quite a number of others, most of which had gone on to college to get qualifications which allowed them to build new futures.

Yet still, there we all were, marooned from the outside world by the marauding hordes of press surrounding our perimeter, all wanting to know just where Steve had taken his victim, and yet none believing the truth when we told them … we genuinely had absolutely no more idea than they had!

Chapter Sixteen

Going back in time to that night when Steve had opened Tony's door during the night to allow Chris and a couple of his mates in, the poor fellow got the shock of his life when he found himself unceremoniously taken from his bed, thrown a set of old clothes to put on, and escorted forcefully outside, pushed over the garden wall, and bundled blindfolded into the back of a van.

"What's going on, where are you taking me, and why this time of night? This isn't what you said we'd be doing; and anyway, who are these men and why have I been blindfolded?"

Steve grinned at Chris who was clearly enjoying getting back to the excitement of their past lives in the para's,

"Will you just sit still, shut up and stop asking questions man? You know what's going on, you're coming to spend time on the streets; we're going in the dark to keep the press from seeing; oh... and as for who these men are, I really think you'd rather not know if you value surviving in one piece mate!"

Tony visibly shuddered at that last remark, while Steve, Chris and the others tried to control their amusement at his obvious discomfort. He'd built his reputation on always being the one to put others on the spot, and to make them feel uncomfortable, and now the tables had been turned completely, he was clearly not happy. For the rest of the journey, which he estimated must have taken getting on for about three to four hours, he did as he'd been told and just sat quietly. He would have probably gone to sleep under different circumstances, but this was not like the journeys he was used to, where he could just sit back and sleep while his chauffer drove smoothly along. This was a rough ride in the back of an uncomfortable old van, surrounded by a gang of, what to him appeared to be, some sort of ruffians or thugs. For all he knew his life could be at risk. This Lockett man, as he saw it, would take little to blow a fuse, and he really knew now that he didn't want to be around if that happened! But just wait, he thought to himself, until we get back. It'll be a different story when I get back on my programme and expose him for what he really is, a brut with no morals or limits to the depths he'll go to! Really not much more than a criminal.

When the van did finally stop he found himself bundled out the back of it, where for a while after he'd found his cramped legs beginning to regain their feeling, he could hear Steve thanking the other men for their help, but it wasn't until they had driven off that his blindfold was removed. He found himself standing in the corner of what was clearly a car park of a sizeable shopping complex. His first thought turned to his lack of breakfast. Surely that would be the first thing on the agenda after the early start and long journey.

At this suggestion Steve laughed,

"Ok, are you buying?"

Tony, not having given thought to that, felt in the pockets of his rather tatty gear he was wearing. Then he looked at Steve and said,

"Ha, ha; you know I can't. That's why you gave me this disgusting old rubbish to wear. No, you'll have to pay for both of us."

"Well, I don't know how you think I'm any better off than you? This is life on the streets mate. You said you were ready to take it on. I suggest you go over there to that snack van and try asking for a hot drink at least."

Tony threw him a dirty look, but walked off in the direction of the van, sure he could charm a couple of cups of tea or coffee if nothing else. Surely nobody could deny them that if they knew they were so hard up. How wrong he was? Barely had he thrown his best smile at the woman serving there and asked her to be kind to a couple of poor, penniless chaps, than she threw him a dirty look and threatened to throw a jug of water over them if they didn't clear off!

This came as a complete shock to a man who was used to always getting anything he asked for. He tried to appeal to her better nature, but it seemed she didn't have one. She picked up the jug and took aim … Tony just managed to back off far enough to avoid a soaking. Steve did his very best not to laugh, but could only do this by turning his back.

"Tough mate; you win some, you lose some, and you clearly lost that time. Better luck next time."

"Glad you enjoyed the joke Lockett. What makes you think you could do better then?"

"That's the whole point of the exercise; I doubt I could. Doubt anyone in our position could come to that. It's down to how people look on the likes of us."

Tony threw him a questioning look,

"What do you mean, 'the likes of us'?"

Steve heaved a sigh before saying,

"Look at yourself in that shop window man. You're just another homeless tramp to the likes of her, not some poncey TV presenter." Then added, "And by the way, for the purposes of this adventure, my name is Joe, not Steve Lockett, do you understand?"

Still not convinced things could possibly be as hard as Steve was making out, none the less he went along with calling Steve Joe, and for Steve to call him Bill, all for the purpose of hiding their true identity.

They walked on away from the retail park and toward the road leading toward what was clearly a large city, but he couldn't be sure at that point exactly where. Coming to a bus stop there he obviously assumed they would jump on one shortly, but then was reminded that without money this was out of the question. Not a happy man but trying not to show this to Steve, he asked how far they had to go.

"Well, that depends where you reckon on spending the night. It's getting pretty cold and a bit damp now, so we need to give it some thought before it gets worse."

Throwing a dirty look at Steve, Tony retaliated with,

"I thought the idea was for you to show me this fantasy world you're always talking about. I've not seen much of it yet."

Trying not to look as aggravated as he felt right then, Steve just turned his back and walked on, saying,

"Oh, don't you worry; you'll see plenty of that over the next days. By the time you get back to your cushy life you'll see just how different it is for folks without your luxury."

Eventually they reached the outskirts of town. Tony took the risk of speaking to his, obviously reluctant, companion, to ask what they needed to do to get food as they'd had nothing since the previous evening. Steve pointed across the road to a burger bar,

"See all those folks going in and out over there? What you have to do is go and sit by the door and try your luck at asking for one of them to get you one. Then we can share it."

Tony looked horrified,

"What, you expect me to sit and beg for food from strangers? You must be mad Loc ... Joe! I can't do that. There must be a better way?"

Steve shook his head and assured him it was that or go hungry!

"I'd sooner go hungry than beg off strangers thank you," Tony threw at him.

"Ok, if you're ok with that it's fine by me. You do get used to going hungry after a while," was Steve's answer, "Rain's coming down harder now. I suggest we find somewhere to bed down for the night. Look, there's another bus shelter over there. Looks a good bet. Besides, if we get over there now the toilets next to it'll be open still."

"Won't it be a bit cold in there? And anyway, what if they're not open?"

Trying hard not to let a broad grin spread across his face, Steve agreed that, yes, of course it would be cold; and as for what to do if the toilets were locked,

"You see the field behind them? Just if you need a descent size leaf to ... well use your imagination man, just watch out for nettles!"

This was enough to make Tony step it out briskly to ensure reaching the conveniences before they were locked for the night! Little did he realise that Steve had been pulling his leg as they were not locked for another hour! Even so, he really could not believe Steve didn't have food of some sort or other which he'd produce once he'd made his point; but he soon found how wrong he was with this assumption! All Steve did produce from his tatty old rucksack was a couple of equally tatty sleeping bags, the same two we'd used all those years ago. Though they were clean, both were obviously well worn, but none the less serviceable. When Tony looked at his in disgust Steve took it back.

"Fine, if it's not good enough, all the better for me. I'm not too proud to use an extra layer. I reckon it'll turn pretty cold later."

Tony tried to make out he was tough enough to cope. Pulling his coat tight around him he turned his back on Steve and tried hard to ignore this remark, but not much more than an hour later he was clearly regretting his decision. As it happened, Steve had been expecting this, and so had been keeping a surreptitious watch of him. Much as he disliked this chap, he knew it was his responsibility to keep him, if not comfortable, at least reasonable safe.

"Here, stop being so stubborn mate. This is no time for being too proud to accept what's on offer. You'll be glad you did by the morning, believe me."

Reluctantly, 'Bill' took the bag from him and, though he wouldn't have admitted to it, was secretly extremely glad he had by the next morning. That night he was really too cold to get a great deal of proper sleep, just cat naps. When daybreak came he began to wonder what would happen this day for food. Surely they were not going without food again? Surely this Lockett character was exaggerating just to make his point? He began to consider making out that he had seen enough to take the point; after all, when he got back to civilisation there would be nothing stopping him from spinning the story his way. It would be for the audience to decide which one of them was telling the truth. And if he could push it hard enough he could paint Lockett in a very poor light.

At least he found Steve did give him the 'luxury' of using the newly opened toilets to relieve himself and splash some water over his face. This was the first time he could remember not getting the luxury of a good, hot shower and shave. As he came out of the building he was met by Steve at the door.

"Come on mate; we have a lot to cover before your education is done. That was just your first lesson on sleeping rough. There's still a lot for you to experience before you'll get the true meaning of homelessness, rather than the one you think you know."

"Ok, so what's next? Suppose you're going to starve me again to make it look good eh? I can't believe we couldn't have brought enough cash to at least feed ourselves."

Steve threw him a look of impatience but managed to fight back the urge to throw back the first answer which came to mind, not wishing to scare the fool away too soon! Instead he explained that, if they needed money, it was another lesson for his companion to learn.

"It's like this 'Bill', if you want food you either have to scrounge it from someone, or find a way to get cash to buy it. You didn't seem so keen on begging for food last night, so perhaps you'd be happier asking for a handout of cash to buy it with?"

"You must be joking if you reckon I'd do either. Anyway, why me? Why don't you show me how it's done?"

"Because that would be defeating the object. You're supposed to be finding out for yourself. See that bakers shop there? Go and try asking in there."

Reluctantly Tony strolled off across to the shop Steve had pointed to. To Steve's surprise, he came back with a small paper bag in his hand and a grin on his face which clearly said,

"See, you're not the only one who can cope."

"Ok, what did they give you then mate?"

Tony proudly opened the bag to reveal its content of two bread rolls, unbuttered, and a small piece of rather dried up cheese! Unfortunately his feeling of pride soon died when he tried to bite into the roll, just to find it was drastically stale. Even more so when he found green mould edging the cheese he'd been so looking forward to.

"Damn! They can't expect us to eat this rubbish surely?" He threw it down in disgust.

Steve laughed out loud, picked it up, scraped the mould off the cheese with his trusty old knife, took a bite from his piece of roll, and ate it with relish! Peter looked on in disgust!

Chapter Seventeen

They say 'pride comes before a fall,' and as Tony was to find, pride can also come before starvation and exposure! Steve was quick to point out that what they'd been given was obviously left over from the previous day. It was hardly likely they would give away their fresh produce so soon after opening after all.

As the day progressed Steve led his companion around the town, and as they turned each corner there seemed to Tony to be those he'd called 'dregs' of society squatting in shop doorways or on corners rattling tins at passers-by in the hope of getting money.

"So how do you know they really need it … they're not just begging as an excuse for not working?"

Steve stopped for a while,

"Ok, I'll give you that. Of course there are plenty of that sort, real lazy buggers, but you need to get a clearer picture to understand. That chap over there for instance, would you say he's a scrounger or genuine?"

Tony looked across at the chap Steve had pointed to,

"Looks fit to work to my mind."

Steve led him across to the fellow in question.

"Mind if we join you," And without waiting for a reply sat down with him.

Steve offered him the last of the cheese, which was gladly accepted. Carefully coaxing this chap into conversation, Tony sat quietly and listened as he explained he was still looking for work to earn enough to get back off the streets.

"Surely there's something available in a place this big? What sort of work do you want mate?"

The poor chap looked in amazement at Tony for a second or two before looking from him to Steve as if asking if his companion was for real.

Steve heaved a sigh before grinning at the poor chap, and explaining that 'Bill' was new to this game.

"He's got a lot to learn. Only just got the push from his work and kicked out the flat that went with it last week. He thinks he can walk into another job that easy. You gonna tell him or shall I?"

The man grinned at Steve, realising that he was clearly more streetwise of the two.

"Tell you what," he said to Tony, "There's a job centre just round the corner there. Bet you can't get them to give you a start at any job anywhere. I'd say I'll buy dinner if you win, but that'd be wishful thinking."

Steve could see the indignation in his companion's eyes, but did a good job of hiding the amusement he felt. When Tony decided to take up the challenge and headed off round the corner to find the job centre, he stayed for a minute or two to chat to the fellow, and it was soon clear that this was yet another of those he had tried so hard to tell Tony about having found himself in really hard times through no fault of his own.

Within a relatively short space of time a rather angry looking Tony came back around the corner to join them.

"Well; how did you get on? When do you start work?"

Their new friend waited for the answer he knew was to come.

"Well, I remembered what you told me not to say 'Joe', but even so I gave them a clear picture of some of the things I had experience of."

"Well? And how did that go down?" Steve asked him.

"They said they'd have no trouble finding me work."

"So?" asked the other chap.

"Well, it was fine until I had to …"

"Had to what, come on, tell us something we don't already know."

Steve stood face to face, eye to eye, almost daring him to wriggle out of telling the truth.

"Ok, if you must know, it was going fine until they found I didn't have a permanent address, after that they tore the forms up and said get one first then come back."

Their new acquaintance laughed and said,

"So tell me now; just how are you planning on paying rent on a place with no regular income. Looks like I'm not buying dinner after all mate."

Seeing both men taking such obvious entertainment at his expense just served to aggravate Tony further. Without another word he turned his back on them and walked away down the road. Steve stopped for long enough to wish their new friend well in his search for help in his dilemma, but then as he walked away, found he couldn't do so without turning back to give him a card with details of Lansdown on and a suggestion to contact that number! He knew he must stop doing this now funds were so badly depleted, but then neither could he bring himself to walk away from someone so obviously down on his luck.

"Sounds a bit grand for the likes of me though I reckon, ain't it mate?"

Without letting on that he owned the place, Steve quickly reassured him that it was run especially for the likes of him.

"Do you really reckon they'll take me in?"

By this time Steve was already walking off after Tony.

"Sure they will pal. Just wave that card at the woman in charge, Mel, and I reckon she'll find somewhere for you."

By the time he turned the corner round which Tony had gone just that few minutes ago, he was immediately aware of a rowdy scrap going on not so far along the road. It didn't take many seconds for him to realise that the victim of the pretty rough attack taking place was Tony! Clearly both men responsible for this were a little high on drugs of some sort and had taken him for a down-and-out. They had decided it would be good sport to take turns pushing him around and calling him names. As Steve approached they had pushed him to the ground and it was clear to Steve that he was totally unable to defend himself from their attack.

"Hey you lot, get off him and pick on someone your own size."

Both men stopped pulling Tony about to look in Steve's direction. Seeing what they assumed to be another tramp by his appearance, grinning at one another, they pushed Tony away and walked threateningly toward Steve.

"Oh, you mean like you eh? Fancy your chances against two of us do you?"

Steve stood his ground with a sarcastic grin creeping across his face. He'd like to have said just how much the frustration of dragging around a wimp like Tony was getting to him, and left him to fight his own battles, but instead he couldn't resist the chance to take them up on their offer of a little welcome exercise!

""Yes, why not? There's nothing like a bit of exercise to set you up for the day. Come on then lads … let's see what you're made of."

This was not the reaction they were expecting at all. Both stopped in their tracks and looked from one to another. Clearly they were bewildered by Steve's response to their challenge … was he bluffing, or was he for real? Ok, he was a pretty tough looking geezer, but there was two of them, and he was only a tramp after all. If they backed down now it would do nothing for their reputation.

A brief nod of the head between them and they both rushed Steve together. Before they'd barely made contact with him they found themselves flat on their backs at his feet. Steve offered them a hand each, apparently to get up, but as they made use of this they were surprised to find that all this did was flip each in turn and return them back to the ground at his feet!

"Now if that's the best you can do I suggest you go and find a job to earn your living, instead of thinking you can go around showing disrespect to your elders like that. There's no telling what harm you'll get in doing that. Now clear off both of you before I get warmed up and teach you a lesson in manners."

Scrambling to their feet, both men took off like a pair of frightened rabbits, looking back just briefly enough to be sure their antagonist wasn't following them! Tony watched them go with a feeling of relief before turning back to Steve who was watching with obvious amusement, and saying with a righteous tone to his voice,

"There, you can't tell me that's how everyone treats your down and outs? And it's pretty clear they were on drugs too."

"As I told you at the start, there's all sorts out here, just like it is in your cosy little world no doubt. Some who are genuinely in need of help ... like the other chap we saw earlier who never asked for anything, but accepted a bit of mouldy old cheese. Then there's the likes of those two hooligans, they're just out for an easy life at someone else's expense but could probably get work if they wanted it. But, like quite a lot of people, they have no respect or sympathy for those who can't ... They're probably off down the nearest pub now on their way home, or taking more of whatever they've already had. The other poor chap will be sleeping rough like we did last night. Difference being, we can go home if it gets too much ... he clearly can't. "

It was clear Tony was still not entirely convinced. Steve walked on from where they'd been standing and headed further into a more built up and populated area. By this time there was so much hustle and bustle, Tony felt he'd like nothing better than to be tucked away in the cosy protection of his studio. By this time of morning he would normally have had his fill of cooked breakfast and be on at least his second coffee of the day. It seemed more than he dared do to ask Steve about food, it was obvious that would be a waste of breath. Eventually Steve stopped at a small bench near a group of shops.

"Now what are we supposed to do? Sit here and beg I suppose?"

Tony's voice couldn't hide the sarcasm he was feeling. Steve chose not to waste his efforts answering such a contemptuous question. He just glared at him and told him to just,

"Sit down and shut up man! All you need to do is use your eyes and ears. Be observant. Try watching others instead of expecting everyone to watch you all the time."

After they'd sat there for twenty minutes or so Tony gradually became aware of the different attitudes of people to them. He noticed that on the whole there were about three types of these; there were just a few who obviously were sympathetic towards them, even offering money (which Steve quickly refused asking for a hot drink or sandwich instead); then there were some who rushed past, trying hard not to look in their direction; but then there were some who glared at them as if they were disgusted at the cheek of such 'tramps' having the nerve to even be seen in 'their' town! Some of these sort even had the audacity to say just that to their faces.

It was just as Tony was trying to cope with these attitudes that came the absolute limit to what he'd expected. He'd noticed a couple of police constables heading in their direction and assumed they were coming to stop these abusive sorts from causing trouble, but this was not the case. They did come over, but they had come to move the two 'vagrants', as they saw them, from the bench, and preferably as far from the town centre as possible! Tony tried to question them as to why he had no right to sit on the bench, but it soon became clear that they considered it their duty to clear the place of any 'undesirables', and that included these two.

Chapter Eighteen

"I reckon we've covered a fair bit of ground today. Come on, let's go and look for somewhere to bed down again."

Tony looked in horror at his companion.

"What do you mean, bed down? We've barely eaten more than the odd sandwich. And surely we don't have to spend another night in a bus shelter do we?"

"Your guess is as good as mine mate; I've never been around this area before. Come on."

So saying he marched off following a road which obviously led out of town and into a quieter, residential area. When Tony asked hopefully if they were going to find a b&b, all Steve could do was roar with laughter and ask,

"Ok, so what do we pay for it with … or are you up to doing a flit without paying and risking being arrested?"

They walked on in silence until Steve spotted a familiar looking sight, an allotment. Ok, he thought, not the one he'd helped the old boy with before when he was sleeping rough, but might be an education for his 'pupil' in how to find food! Leaving a nervous Tony standing guard at the gate, he sneaked across to a patch where there were potatoes growing. Using his knife (the large, ex-army one), he managed to extract a couple of descent sized potatoes each, make good the ground to hide where he'd been, and make his getaway unseen!

"Now what? Do we eat them raw," Tony muttered with obvious disdain.

"You can if you like, you would if you were starving, believe me. But I reckon we can find a better way. See those woods further up the road? That's where we're heading."

Totally bewildered but so hungry by this time he'd accept anything, Tony willingly followed Steve off up the road and into the wood they'd seen in the distance. By this time he felt dirty, starving, and most of all exhausted. The argumentative attitude he'd displayed all day had finally worn off. Steve had noticed this but said nothing. Perhaps it would be a quicker lesson to teach than he'd expected, but then he should have guessed this fellow had never had to deal with hardship before.

He led him deep into the wood to be away from interference from anyone else. After collecting wood from around a suitable camping spot, Steve showed Tony how to make a fire with enough to warm them. Once there were enough hot embers around the fire he put the newly acquired potatoes into it and, turning them occasionally, left them to bake. While this was happening he took a groundsheet from his rucksack and laid it out to put their sleeping bags onto. Luckily the weather was dry that night, but as he explained, had it rained they would have needed to attach the groundsheet to the trees or bushes to give some sort of covering. Having organised the camp and cooking, he turned to Tony, who had been standing around with a bewildered expression on his face.

"Right, now get over here and sit yourself down now."

To Tony this sounded more like an order than an invitation! He immediately did as he was told.

"Right now, when we set out on this journey I set myself aims at certain things you needed to learn about your so called 'dregs'. Let's see how we're getting on. First, how are you finding sleeping rough, either in town, like last night, or like you're going to do tonight?"

"Well, obviously I'm not keen; who would be? Of course I prefer being safe in my own bed. Don't you then?"

Steve heaved a sigh of frustration,

"Just answer my questions, then I'll tell you how I feel. So, what about food?"

Tony gave Steve a look of disdain,

"Food, what bloody food? We've barely eaten since we left home. Now you expect me to survive on a couple of spuds ... stolen ones at that!"

"No mate, I don't expect anything. You eat them or go without. All I want you to do is see just how hard it is to find food without money, how to get money without work, and then just how to find work without a place to live. From then it's a vicious circle as you need to earn enough to pay rent or the whole cycle goes round again. Surely you see that by now?"

Not really too keen to be proved wrong, or worse still a fool, Tony tried hard to find a different angle to look from.

"Yes ok, I'll give you that with some of them, but surely that's no reason to take drugs and drink like a lot you see around?"

Steve put down the potatoes he was extracting from the embers, heaved yet another sigh louder than the first, before shaking his head in despair and saying,

"Ok, I can see you've made up your mind to prove my life's work a waste of time haven't you? You're just being plain bloody minded if you ask me. Ok, tomorrow I'll find you a few of those sort, then I'll really show you the reason for what they do. I can tell you now, if you had their lives you'd be just as happy to turn to drink and drugs."

Cutting the potatoes in half he handed one to Tony (though he felt more like throwing it at him!), and said,

"There, get that inside you, and don't waste it... not even the skin. You'll be glad of it by this time tomorrow."

"What do you suggest I eat it with?"

With a shake of his head, Steve picked up a stick from the ground, ran his knife down it to shape it into a flat utensil of sorts and said,

"So sorry Sir, the butler forgot to pack the silver. Now, get on and eat it or I'll have them all!"

The rest of the evening was passed in relative silence. Tony could sense Steve's patience was wearing thin, so he sat and ate without a word. Luckily the night stayed dry, which meant they had the groundsheet to keep the sleeping bags off the slightly damp ground. When, at Steve's suggestion, they turned in pretty early while the fire was still burning a little, Tony was glad of its warmth to help take his mind from the many assorted woodland noises. He would have liked to ask how safe they were ... were there any creatures in the wood to be scared of? But he knew this would just show him up for the coward he was. And so, pulling the bag up as far as possible to drown out such noises, he was soon able to concentrate on one noise only ... Steve's snoring!

Chapter Nineteen

Much to his surprise Tony had eventually conquered his nerves and dropped off to sleep. The next thing he was aware of was Steve standing over him bashing a stick on the side of one of the tin mugs he'd brought along, and saying,

"Teas up. Hope you like mushrooms for breakfast."

He yawned, rubbed his eyes and looked to where Steve was now sitting by a freshly lit fire. In his hand he held a small pan in which there were a few small mushrooms gently cooking over the fire. Perhaps this was going to be an easier day he thought. At least it was looking promising with a good breakfast to start the day. He stretched, climbed out of his bag, and went over to the fireside.

"No chance of a rasher of bacon I suppose?"

Steve looked round at him in disbelief,

"Well, not unless you fancy butchering a pig first. I think we passed some down the road a way. I'll lend you this," And as he said this he held out his knife!

Seeing his companion recoil in disgust at the thought of doing such a thing brought a broad grin across Steve's face. He hadn't had so much fun since the days so long ago now when he'd tried suggesting Mel should go and milk a cow in a farmer's barn to supply their breakfast. But there, he thought, it just separates those who've never been hungry from those who have.

"No, I thought not. This is survival at the sharp end you might say. There's always food to forage for in a place like this if you know where to look. There's a hot drink here for you."

Tony picked up the cup, grateful for something to warm both his cold hands and his inside.

"I take it there's no milk either?"

"Sorry mate, it's too far to walk back to that field of cows. And anyway, it doesn't go well with that tea."

"What sort of tea is it then?"

Again Steve supressed his amusement,

"Nettle tea; and don't pull a face like that! You'd soon be glad of anything you could find if you were living this life for real."

By now Tony was learning that it was probably best to go along with Steve as much as possible and not to incur his wrath. He decided that perhaps he should make an attempt to keep things on an even keel, but none the less, watch out for ways to prove his point … after all, there must be plenty if he could just find them.

They ate the mushrooms, packed up their camp into Steve's rucksack, and set off onward toward the next town. It came as a great relief to Tony when Steve managed to cadge a lift in a lorry not far along the road. He didn't want to say, but he was more used to being chauffeured around than hiking everywhere, but neither did he feel up to a long walk, and certainly not at Steve's pace! When they were eventually dropped off it seemed to Tony to be a pretty run-down area. There seemed to be unused factory buildings on the outskirts of an area of rough looking terraced housing, and populated with a variety of, what to Tony looked, a pretty miserable bunch of people. He couldn't help thinking to himself that this is just the type of place he'd expect to find the sort of drunks, druggies and layabouts he felt sure would prove him right.

Steve stopped at one point, turning to look into an alley behind a couple of rows of houses.

"Wait; we need to go back. Did you see that kid down there?"

Tony had to admit to not doing so, but Steve was already heading back the way he'd pointed, so all he could do was follow. Standing, or rather leaning, against a wall, even Tony could tell she was high on something, probably drugs (which he felt sure would prove his point). Steve signalled for Tony to stay where he was while he approached her quietly.

At first she seemed unaware of his presence, but as he got closer to her she looked up at him with a scared look on her face. He could see she would like to have run off but could barely stand without the support of the wall behind her.

"It's ok, don't be scared dear, I just thought you looked in need of some help."

She turned a very puzzled and disbelieving face to him,

"Why should you care? Anyway, who are you and what do you want?"

As she said this she lost her balance, and would have ended on the ground just then had he not put out an arm to catch her.

"Here, let me help you. My name is Joe, and I don't want anything. What's your name?"

"Sarah, I'm feeling ..." and before she could say more, and just missing 'Joe', she threw up at his feet!

"God; how old are you girl? And what've you been taking?"

Between further bouts of throwing up, Sarah managed to get out enough to tell Steve she was just eighteen, and had been smoking weed. When he quizzed her for how long, she told him this was for the last four months. He'd just begun to ask her why she'd started when a scruffy looking chap appeared round the corner to see what was happening.

"Hey mate, what is it you're after there, the gear or the girl?"

His face turned to Steve with an ugly smirk across it, clearly feeling he had plenty to offer.

"Oh I see. That's your game eh? Reckon I'd get both for the same price anyway seeing as she's taken the gear already. Was that your idea?"

With an even uglier smirk he winked at Steve and said,

"Well, it's having it that makes her more obliging, if you know what I mean. In fact she'll no doubt manage you both by now. So, are you ready to pay me first mate?"

"Oh yes, don't worry. I'll pay you … well over the top at that."

So saying Steve took a step toward him and gave vent to the sheer anger sweeping through him at that moment. His fist landed on the fellow so hard Tony was convinced he'd killed him!

"What did you do that for," piped up Tony, "You could have killed him?"

"What you mean is, I 'should' have killed him! It's the likes of that creep that get these kids hooked on the stuff just to make money. Now come and help me get her up. We're taking her with us."

"But if she's a druggie what's the point? Doesn't that prove what I've been saying?"

Steve shook his head in disbelief. How could anyone be so blind, he wondered? Without bothering to answer such a stupid question, he scooped up the girl in his arms and walked back in the direction they'd come. He didn't stop until they were well away from where they'd met Sarah, and then he found an old disused factory unit which was open. There he put her down gently on the ground and gave her a drink from his flask. Her first reaction to this was to repeat throwing up as before. Though this disgusted Tony, Steve knew that this would help to wash the drugs from her temporarily.

"When did you last eat Sarah?" he asked.

"I'm not sure ... probably yesterday, or maybe the day before ... I'm not sure."

Steve shook his head and said to her,

"And it's being hungry makes you take the drugs he dishes out eh?"

Sarah nodded, before adding quietly, almost under her breath,

"And it helps with the pain."

Tony couldn't help but see the fury Steve was struggling to hide by turning away from her for a brief instant before turning back to her with a gentle smile on his face,

"Look Sarah, this is my friend Bill. He's perfectly harmless, just a bit ignorant sometimes, but if he stays with you do you promise to stay here for a bit while I go and find some food for us all?"

Though she did give 'Bill' a strange look, she felt that this Joe bloke seemed pretty genuine, so she promised she would, as long as her pimp didn't find her! Steve guaranteed her that there was no chance of that. As Steve glanced back over his shoulder at the two of them sitting like a pair of scared kids in the corner, he wondered just how he was ever going to make the likes of Tony truly understand the hardships which drive the likes of young Sarah to live the way they do; would he ever get them to see the world is far from black and white ... it's made up of as many different colours as a rainbow. Steve himself had grown up believing this, in fact his father, Peter, had encouraged this belief since he was a small boy, bringing him up to make allowances for any he would come into contact with through his lifetime, especially those less fortunate than himself.

Chapter Twenty

Steve was not gone very long. When he did come back he had a bag with three big sausage rolls inside. They were warm and inviting, and he could tell by the way the girl attacked hers that she clearly hadn't eaten for some time. Tony resisted the temptation to ask how he'd come by these, for fear of having it taken away.

"Go steady Sarah, if you eat too quickly you'll make yourself sick again. Just take your time and enjoy it because we don't have money to buy more, so it may be the last you'll get for a while if you stay with us."

"Do you mean you'd let me? What's the catch; I mean, what do you want in return?"

She gave a worried look from one to the other of the two men, a look which showed just how mistrusting she was of them, or any other men come to that. Steve was quick to reassure her that they had no agenda other than to keep her out of the clutches of the likes of the one she'd been with.

"But you're free to go anytime you want to. Just please get some help with the drugs, and stay out of the clutches of that brute."

Steve handed her half of his sausage roll, clearly seeing that she had greater need of it than him. She took his advice and ate this rather slower than the last one! To allow her time to eat without feeling in any way trapped by the two men, Steve signalled Tony to sit just outside the door with him.

"Do you see what happens to the likes of her once these blokes get their teeth into them? They get them hooked on drugs, and from then on they can do what they like with them, either use them as drug mules to cart the stuff around, or even worse, turn them into prostitutes to bring in money. I've seen kids as young as fourteen in that same boat, and nobody gives a damn!"

"So then, what are they doing out on the streets in the first place? Why don't they just go home where they belong?"

Steve shook his head, once more in despair at his companion's lack of understanding. Had he really never given thought to the world outside his own tight little bubble?

"Well, that is assuming they have homes to go home to. In so many cases the younger ones run away from abusive parents. In the case of the older ones like Sarah here, either they've been abused at home, or they've not got a proper home to go to."

"What do you mean, no proper home? They must have come from somewhere?"

"You often find they're kids who've been in care and have nowhere to go when they leave. Don't bother asking why they leave. If you had ever bothered to give it any thought you'd know that, when they reach eighteen they don't qualify for care. Basically they're on their own from then on."

Tony looked in amazement at Steve,

"Surely they can't just kick them out though."

"Oh yes they can, and very often that's just what they have to do. You must understand there's always more coming in at the bottom end to accommodate those at the top. Come on, let's see she's ok in there."

It came as no surprise to Steve to find Sarah curled up asleep under the old coat he'd taken off to put round her shoulders earlier. Now she looked very much the vulnerable, childlike figure, and very much less the drugged up prostitute Tony had assumed her to be. The sight of this transformation couldn't help but start to bring about just a little vision of Steve's world, though he certainly had no intention of admitting defeat at this point. It would do nothing for his reputation after all. No, the least he needed was to hear from her just how she came to be living such a life. Only when he heard it from her own mouth would he believe that what Steve had just told him could be the truth.

It seemed that Steve had managed to convince her that she was safe with them. This was no easy feat after the life she'd been living for the last months. Having had a bite to eat and a warm up, she had allowed herself to curl up and go to sleep. Steve had intended taking Tony even deeper into this world of drugs to show him just how young some of these kids are who get caught up in such lives by these unscrupulous men, but his priority right that minute was to keep at least this one safe. He could see that his explanation to Tony about the care system only being able to provide for them up to the age of eighteen had not been entirely believed. In fact it was not until a good hour or so later, when Sarah woke up, that he was able to ask her about her previous life.

Reluctantly at first, she told them she had been put in care at the age of ten, due to her mother passing away, and her father being both unable and unwilling to look after her. She had been in assorted foster homes for part of the time, but never any one long enough to feel settled. In the last three years leading up to her eighteenth birthday, she had been in a care home. She'd just felt so out of place, so lonely, that she'd gone out most of the time she was able to, and it was then that she'd been approached by the man she'd been with. At first he had seemed really kind and seemed to want to take care of her, but before long he began to introduce her to drugs (on the pretext of making her feel good!).

"But why did you let him push you at men like that?" Tony put to her, "Wasn't it bad enough to take that muck?"

The look Steve threw him quickly stopped him from saying any more. But Sarah answered him none the less,

"I might have been glad of the drugs to blot out what was happening to me, but I still needed to eat sometimes. If I didn't do as he said I got no food and he'd shove me outside to sleep like a bloody dog!"

Throwing Tony a dirty look, Steve growled at him,

"Get outside and wait for me there where you can do less harm. I'll be with you in a minute,"

Tony looked more than a little hurt at being dismissed like a naughty schoolboy, but once again, followed Steve's orders. As she saw him go, a look of panic spread over Sarah's face. What was going to happen now, or worse still were they really going to leave her on her own? She wasn't bothered about that Bill bloke, but there was something about the big fellow, Joe, that had made her feel safe for the first time in ages. Was she wrong to trust him? There again, what would she do now if they were going to go off and leaving her here?

"Don't look so scared Sarah. What the hell you think I'm going to do I'm really not."

"But you're going to leave me here though aren't you? What do I do, where can I go? If I go back he'll beat the shit out of me …"

Steve took hold of her hand and led her back to where she'd been sitting.

"Now, just stop your panicking. I've no intention of leaving you anywhere either that scum bag or anyone like him can get hold of you."

A look of relief mixed with bewilderment swept over her face. Before she had chance to speak again, Steve sat her down, looked her in the eye, and asked,

"If we leave you here just for a while, do you promise you'll wait till we get back? I promise we'll be back in an hour, two at the most. And when we get back we'll bring more food and can go right away from here. You'll never have to see that bugger or anyone like him again," and seeing her hesitation added, "I promise you Sarah. You do believe me don't you?"

He could tell just how much she wanted to believe. He told her he would leave his coat with her to prove it.

"What, this mucky old thing?" She laughed. "Ok, I'll wait, but if you're gone too long I'm off."

"What do you like to eat by the way? Burger do you?"

The smile he threw her was enough to convince her to agree to wait ... well, that and the mention of a burger!

Chapter Twenty-One

Meanwhile, while Steve was out 'on manoeuvres', as he called it when I last saw him, May had settled in beautifully. I was glad to see just how much pleasure she seemed to gain from spending time with Will and Lilly. As she had requested, we sneaked past the press that remained outside (even though they must have known by this time they were wasting their time), and paid a family visit up to the little church on top of the hill, where she pointed out to us where the ashes of all her family, and her husband Peter's family were all buried in adjacent family plots. I had to admit that this was the first time I'd known of this. As I stood with her watching, she quietly reminded me of something she'd asked me to keep in mind; she had said that, when her time came, she was to be buried with Peter Lockett. Now I could see the sheer devotion she held for him, even so long after his death, and just why there was a space right by his side.

The following day she spent time sitting with Will and Lilly in the evening. I had made hot drinks for us all as it was not a particularly warm evening, and while I was doing this Will was going slowly through the sizeable box of things she'd given him to keep for the baby. It amused me to see him rummaging through its contents like a kid at Christmas. Of course, back in his much younger days, he had seen and played with many of the things in there, but it had been so long ago that he could barely remember some of them.

By the time he reached the bottom of the box Will suddenly exclaimed,

"Look Nan, the bottom is full of the books you used to read to me all those years ago!"

May couldn't help a little laugh at his excitement over this.

"Yes dear. If you remember, right from when you were tiny, the only way to keep you still for five minutes was to sit you on my lap and read a book to you. Your little finger would follow mine along the page in an attempt to read the words, and the more colourful the pictures, the more times we had to read the same ones over and over!"

"Now I know why he spends so much time with his head in books," laughed Lilly, "At least I know you'll be good at keeping this one amused."

As she said this she gave her, now sizeable bulge, a gentle pat.

"Oh yes, he'll be good at that. Now, which one was it you always liked best? Ah yes, this one wasn't it?"

May had picked out a particularly colourful little volume from amongst the pile. There was a picture of a brilliantly coloured rainbow right across the cover. She flicked through the pages to refresh her memory. It was clear from the way she looked at this, somewhat well-thumbed volume, that it brought back good memories.

"You do know this was your Dad's book long before it was yours? He was a firm believer in the little Irish leprechauns it talks of, and their idea that the rainbow lets us hold onto our hopes and dreams, and find new beginnings. That was why his Dad, Peter, always called him his little rainbow boy"

"Yes, I think I remember something about that. And what was that about a pot of gold? I'm sure there was something about that too."

"Well, that's what they say. If you can find the end of a rainbow there'll be a pot of gold there. Of course that's supposed to symbolise your dreams coming true." May smiled a contented smile at Will and said,

"I think that living here with you all makes Lansdown Grange my pot of gold; my dreams have truly come true my dears, all we really need is for my rainbow boy to find his pot of gold!"

As I lay in bed that night, feeling a little lost without my dear Steve alongside of me, I couldn't help thinking of what May had said about the Grange being her 'pot of gold', but even more so about the rainbow itself being a symbol of hope, dreams and new beginnings. Strange that this had been so symbolic of the whole life Steve and I had shared together over the years. Perhaps it had been Steve's belief from his childhood book introducing him to the idea of the symbolism of the rainbow which had brought us to where we are now. All we really need if that be the case is to find the pot of gold at the end to enable our dreams to come true! We could certainly do with that right now to keep this particular dream to alive.

Oh well; perhaps it had been rather ambitious to think we could keep it going forever. It would be such a shame if we had to give up on all the work Steve had done so far over the years since we first came here. And then, if we did find we couldn't afford to keep the place going as a rehabilitation centre after all the good work everyone involved had put in over the years, just what would we do with the Grange? It would have been far too big just as a family home in the first place, but even more so after all the additions we've made over the years.

The shame of it was that, since finding he had actually inherited Lansdown, Steve had actually allowed himself to put down roots and settle, giving up on his tendency toward a nomadic life! He had turned the wreck of a place around and made it somewhere to be proud of. You could say that it had been his rainbow which had led him here.

But all his efforts could still come to nothing if we couldn't find support from somewhere, and right now it was beginning to look as if we were fighting a losing battle. Sleep that night became very restless as I worried just what effect it would have on dear Steve if his dreams came crashing down around him after so long!

Chapter Twenty-Two

Steve was quick to usher Tony away from where he'd left Sarah, before she could be even more upset by the attitude of his companion. As he marched him off in the direction of town he was quick to reprimand his companion on his lack of sensitivity. Tony on the other hand found it hard to understand just what he had done so wrong.

"Just show a little understanding man. Surely it's not too much to ask to expect you to think before you speak? Poor kid's had it tough all her life, and then you come along and accuse her of getting into all of that of her own free will! Just try to show a little compassion for goodness sake."

As they came into the more populated part of the town, Steve's ears picked up on a sound of a guitar ... a badly tuned one at that, and the chap playing it was giving a pretty feeble rendition of a couple of the latest hits. This was more than Steve could resist. He strolled right up to the chap and asked (quite politely), could he help to tune up his instrument! Some would possibly have been offended at this, but it did seem that this fellow had absolutely no idea how to do this himself, and so was quite glad of the offer of help. Of course, as soon as he'd actually done this, Steve was more than glad to join the lad in a duet.

Tony watched in astonishment, not having a musical bone in his body, but was even more astonished by the vast amount of money thrown into a box on the ground! Of course, this was not the first time Steve had done this. Many years ago, on the first journey he'd gone on with Mel, they had come across another lad in a similar situation. That lad had been Josh, the very young man who is now head chef at Lansdown Grange. At that time though he had been just another homeless lad trying to earn a few pounds by busking, but not doing particularly well. Even Tony could tell how much better this fellow sounded with Steve alongside to support him, and, though he wouldn't have wanted to acknowledge it, the thought did just flash through his mind that perhaps Steve could have possibly made a living singing, had he chosen to do so.

Before they moved on from him, Steve enquired casually, where did he live? With some reluctance, and only because he assumed by their apparel that they too were rough sleepers, he confided in them that there was a 'half descent' squat on the outskirts of town.

"Would we be welcome pal? Just us two and a girl we've got tagging along with us?"

He asked where this girl was and Steve said he had to go back for her,

"But she's no bother. Just a bit lost, needs keeping away from certain folk, if you know what I mean?"

It was evident that he completely understood what Steve told him. Steve introduced them as Joe and Bill. The lad, Andy, agreed to carry on busking until they got back. He was quick to say not to worry about food. After helping collect such a good amount together just now he would be able to buy their share of supplies for tonight.

As they headed back to fetch Sarah, Tony asked Steve why they were going to this squat.

"Isn't that the next best thing to breaking and entering? These buildings must belong to someone I'd have thought."

"Think man! Most squats are in houses that are standing empty. Meanwhile there are so many out there with nowhere to sleep. Would you begrudge them a roof over their heads? Keep your ears open while we're there ... you might learn something!"

It didn't take them long to get back to the place they had left Sarah. When they opened the door and peered in there was no sign of her, but that didn't surprise Steve. He called out to her quietly,

"Sarah, it's ok, you can come out now, it's just Joe and Bill."

There was a quiet scuffling sound from behind a pile of sacks in the corner. A small, scared looking face slowly appeared from where she'd been hiding. Once she had convinced herself they were who they said they were, she came out slowly from her hiding place, still with Steve's old coat wrapped round her shoulders.

"Thought you'd forgotten me! Did you really mean it when you said I can go with you when you leave here?"

Steve assured her that he had meant it, but that they were staying the other side of town in a squat just for tonight if that was ok with her. It was pretty clear she didn't feel comfortable about that idea, but agreed to on condition 'Joe' didn't let anyone touch her!

"Do you really think I'd do that Sarah? Look, I'm a married man with a son a couple of years or so older than you. Come to that I'll soon be a grandfather! I promised you you'd be safe and I meant it."

Even Tony could see the obvious relief visible on her face. He would hate to have admitted this but he was beginning to feel a respect for this man who he had originally felt such animosity toward. None the less, he knew in his mind that when this 'stupid' expedition came to an end, he just had to find ways to discredit him and prove himself right in his original assumptions. He wished in some ways that Lockett had let him arrange for a film crew to come along. After all, film can always be edited to prove almost anything you wanted it to. Now it was just his word against Steve's.

Though Sarah accepted Steve's word that Andy was quite harmless, she still was not too sure about going into the squat. Unfortunately for her the other occupants were all male. There were three others around a similar age to Andy, but there was also two of similar age to 'Joe' and 'Bill', and it was these two who concerned her the most. After all, the pimp Steve had rescued her from had been more their age. She made up her mind to stick as close to him as possible, just to be on the safe side!

Andy made it his job to introduce everyone. It seemed Steve had already made an impression on him, and this had been spread amongst the others. It was this which persuaded them to accept these new incomers to their place. It seemed they were all there for different reasons. Andy and one of the other younger chaps were struggling to complete college courses, but had found it impossible to pay for accommodation. The other youngster had left home due to abuse from his step-father, preferring to live rough rather than suffer further ill treatment, but once again, found it impossible to find descent employment with no address, and so was just making do with casual labour wherever he could.

The two older men had both been working for one of the firms from the factories where Steve had taken Tony and Sarah earlier, but when the firm had gone bust they had been left, as so often is the case, without the funds to cover rent on the flats they'd lived in. Once again Tony saw just how such events had a way of sending lives into that ever-revolving circle of no job, no rent, no home, and as an end result, no self-pride.

At least, Tony thought to himself, thanks to Steve and this young Andy chap, they had somewhere undercover to spend the night plus enough food to leave him feeling fuller than he'd done since leaving home! Even so, during the course of the two nights Steve chose to remain in that dirty, deserted hovel of a place, he became very aware of the terrible conditions these chaps were living in, and just why this was.

There was no electricity for a start. That meant no light, heat, or cooking facility save that which they had used their ingenuity to organise. The younger amongst them had camping lamps and small camping stoves. The problem with these facilities was that it was difficult to warm, let alone cook, food for everyone without taking so much time and gas which was too expensive to run to. Then of course, for the two students, they needed to find a way to pay to take a little clothing to a launderette to enable them to turn up at college in an acceptable state. This explained the reasoning behind Andy's attempt at busking! The remaining men, so Tony learnt from listening to their conversations with Steve, spent their time on the fruitless search for work ... any work, in their desperate attempt to get back on their feet.

When he woke up the next morning Tony found himself alone with the other squatters. Steve and Sarah were nowhere to be seen. He was about to go into panic mode, thinking he'd been dumped in this awful situation alone, but then one of the men handed him a note which just read,

'Stay where you are until I get back. Gone to find Sarah somewhere safe.'

At least he found that he came to no harm. In fact he was surprised how accommodating everyone was toward him. He'd not surfaced from his sleeping bag when he was handed a very welcome mug of coffee. Andy gave him a couple of slices of bread and butter, but apologised for the lack of facilities to toast this. At first Tony wondered if he was being sarcastic, but then this was a homeless student, not Steve Lockett!

Chapter Twenty-Three

Steve had already planned the early start he'd got off to that morning. One thing he'd kept secret from Tony was the mobile phone hidden away in the bottom of his old rucksack. Of course, he hadn't bargained for having Sarah to deal with. He had had to wake her quietly, so that Tony didn't know what was going on. Even this had its perils; her first reaction to finding a man waking her from her sleep, was to attempt to scream, but Steve was ready for this and quickly put one hand over her mouth whilst whispering reassuring words in her ear at the same time!

As they crept away from the house she was quick to ask him what was happening, where he was taking her, and why they had left Bill behind? Steve insisted on getting away from the area and towards the outskirts of town before finding a suitable wall to sit her down on to explain.

"Now listen carefully Sarah. Now, firstly, my name is not Joe; it's Steve, Steve Lockett. You've probably not heard of me, but my wife, Mel and myself run a sort of safe house for homeless and those in need of rehab."

He fished into his pocket and produced out a card with details of Lansdown Grange, and showing his and Mel's names on one side and a photo of the Grange on the other.

"Bloody hell man! Are you trying to tell me you live there?"

Steve grinned, he could barely believe it himself even after so long.

"Yes, left to me by my old Granny. Not a bad little shack is it?"

"You must have been a real grannies boy to get that."

Steve had never given thought to just how he would have got on with the late Mrs Stanwick, but now it occurred to him for the first time that perhaps he just might have got along with her better than he'd always imagined. After all, she certainly couldn't be held responsible for her son, Henry, raping his poor mother, May. And anyway, the fact that she'd chosen to leave the Grange to him, an illegitimate grandson she had never met, rather than Henry's legitimate son Luke, showed her to be a lady of strong beliefs in right and wrong. In that respect perhaps, Steve thought, they may have got along pretty well.

"Well, as it happens, I never got to meet her ... but now I come to think of it, it's a shame I didn't. Anyway, I think it would be a good place for you to go right now. I have a mate, Chris, coming here in a few minutes. He's bringing a few people to help me."

Before she could ask what with he continued,

"What I'd like is if you'd go back with him to my place and stay there with Mel until I get back."

He could see her expression change at the thought of being packed off with a strange man, and any other time Steve would have agreed that Chris was a very strange man, but he resisted the temptation to joke about it this time! By the time Chris did pull up with his van, she was surprised to see about five people, in assorted types of outfits, pile out and greet Steve. Having acknowledged them first, he went to speak to this chap she guessed to be Chris. Like Steve, Chris was equally tall and tough looking, though clean shaven. All she overheard of the conversation between them was Chris saying something about 'can't keep collecting more waifs and strays', by which she guessed she was the one he was talking of.

Steve beckoned for her to come over and meet Chris. She felt nervous ... could she trust him; Steve had told her he was ok, but after all, he was still a man, and her experience of that sex had never been a good one. If he thought of her as just a 'waif' or 'stray', as he put it, could she expect him to treat her any differently to the men she'd been used to in the past?

Nervously she walked across to stand close to Steve. Chris noticed her nervousness and laughed,

"I see old smooth talking Steve's got you under his spell like he does all the girls,"

And then, seeing a quick flash of alarm in her eyes adds,

"I mean in a good way dear. Believe me, he wouldn't hurt a fly ... well, not a female one at any rate! You'll be just as safe with me too, Sarah isn't it? Come on, I'll take you to meet Mel. You'll like her. I'm pretty keen on her myself, but she won't have none of me all the time old tough-guy here is about!"

Steve gave him a friendly slap on his back as they turned away and just laughed,

"She wouldn't have you anyway old man."

With just a little encouragement from Steve, Sarah allowed Chris to lead her back to his van, and with one last slightly worried look as they drove away, they headed off in the distance on the hope of a better, safer life, and a chance to kick off the drugs once and for all.

After seeing them off Steve rallied his small band of troops, all residents of the Grange. He had briefed them before leaving home with instructions as to what he needed them to do. Now, thanks to Chris, he kitted them up with small hidden cameras, so that they were able to film the happenings unfolding before them. All of these having found their way to Steve's door for all the usual reasons, were very well aware of people's attitudes to folk unfortunate enough to be living rough for whatever these reasons were. The plan was just to be absolutely certain that there was no way Tony could deny the reaction, and therefore the humiliation, shown toward and by him as he was now in that situation himself. He then headed back to the squat to collect the, by that time rather anxious Tony.

Though Andy had been kind and once more given him a ration of bread and butter, this time with a piece of cheese to go with it, He still felt uneasy until he saw Steve heading up the road in their direction. Whatever he was going to have to face this day, though he would have denied it if asked, he knew in his mind that he would feel safer in the company of this man who he'd originally disliked. Now, not only was he beginning to feel a certain respect for him, but in many ways couldn't help envying the strength and self-confidence of the man.

"Right, come on man, we'd better get going I suppose. Thanks for putting us up chaps, it's really appreciated," Steve said, just turning back at the door, out of sight of Tony to hand Andy a bundle of five tenner's to share between them all!

When Andy went to question this Steve just whispered, "Get a look at BBC, ten a.m. Monday after next if you get chance." Then they were gone.

When Steve went out to where he was waiting, the first thing Tony said to him was,

"I see you've dumped the girl, suppose there's not much you can do once they get hooked on that stuff is there?"

He'd barely got the words out before he regretted them. The glare Steve gave him quickly warned him to stop before he got his head bitten off yet again. They walked on in silence for a few more yards before he spoke again.

"So what exciting things have you got planned for me today then?"

Steve could sense that, although Tony was attempting to put on a nonchalant attitude, underneath this it was clear that his original bluster and show of pride had given way to, hopefully, something akin to understanding of just how this side of the population really live! None the less, little did Tony know that this day was going to completely shake any preconceived ideas which he may still be harbouring.

Having placed his 'spies' from the Grange at suitable spots around the area, he was shortly going to disappear from Tony's view, yet Tony would never truly be out of his sight. With this in mind they hadn't gone so far before Steve told him to carry on the way they were going, and he would catch up after a quick 'convenience stop'. Tony did as he was told, but after a while stopped to wait. It was while he was stood on a corner waiting for Steve that Tony had his encounter with a smart, middle aged man who went to walk on by, but then stopped, looked down his nose at Tony, before coming over and handing him a little loose change,

"You poor chap. Go and get yourself a hot drink," and adding with true conviction, "It'll do you more good than booze you know."

Well! ... Tony was so put out, he wanted to throw it back in the chaps face, but then saw his reflection in a shop window. This convinced him that perhaps he should accept being taken for a tramp, but he was far from happy about it. He'd really begun to notice peoples different reactions to rough sleepers, and it wasn't a feeling he liked.

No, he thought, he'd go back to the toilets Steve had gone to. He'd been gone some time now. But then, when he got there, there was no sign of his companion. The place was empty. He called out, opened each cubicle door, but no sign! He stood in the doorway briefly, wondering where Steve had gone. Just as he was about to give up and go looking for him, an older man he'd not seen sooner came along. Looking from left to right in a very shifty manner, the man sidled up to Tony in a very suspicious way and said in a loud whisper,

"You looking for some gear mate? I can let you have some good stuff at a good price; you won't get better."

It was only then that he remembered Steve telling him about the dealers who would hang around such places ... conveniently so that their clients could shoot up!

He barely stopped long enough to say no before taking off like a scared rabbit!

Chapter Twenty-Four

Unsure just what he should do next, for a while Tony wandered off up the road toward the few shops that seemed to be open. Perhaps Steve had gone there in search of supplies for the day; perhaps he'd assumed Tony had wandered in that direction? He walked as far as the crossroads in the centre of the town, but still there was no sign of his protector, and he was beginning to feel decidedly agitated. After a while just standing around, he began to wonder if he dared go into a shop, or even ask someone, if he could use a phone. He knew he had no money to pay them, but he felt sure that, if he introduced himself, someone would recognise him and be glad to help. With this in mind he approached the next man who came along.

"Good morning Sir," The man stopped and gave him a very suspicious look, "I was just wondering, would you allow me to use your mobile just for a brief minute please?"

The man looked him up and down in what could only be described as disgust!

"I beg your pardon, what makes you think I'd hand my phone over to the likes of you?"

Tony felt he had to do or say something quickly, or it would be too late. He felt in his pockets for something to identify himself, but of course he had nothing. Damn, he thought, why ever did he let Lockett leave him in this position?

"I'm not what you think I am. I'm really a TV presenter, but I ..."

"Yes, and I'm Lord mayor of London! Now clear off before I call the police and get you arrested."

Tony wanted to argue his case, but could see the man meant what he'd said. He knew there was no way to convince him otherwise. Reluctantly he had to turn away and look around for another answer to his predicament

As it happened Steve had been watching this encounter from a distance. Unlike the last couple, this one had not been one of his people, so he'd been on stand-by to come to the rescue if Tony had found himself in trouble. In fact, he found it quite amusing, satisfying even, to see poor Tony unable to make someone believe he was who he said he was. If nothing else it proved that the old adage, 'clothes maketh the man', certainly does hold true. For all the man's swank when he was in the studio dressed in expensive suits, put out on the streets in the clothes of any old rough sleeper, it brought all down to the same level.

As Steve stayed watching from a distance he couldn't believe the stupidity of the man! After his last encounter, he walked straight up to a woman who was just coming out of the bank! He'd barely opened his mouth to ask her for a use of her phone when, not stopping to listen properly to what he was saying, she turned and ran straight back into the bank, screaming as she went that there was a tramp outside trying to rob her!

Oh hell, Steve thought, she was certainly not one of his people so now there would be big trouble! He had to do something quickly. Without hesitation he dashed across the road to a bemused looking Tony, grabbed him roughly by the arm, and dragged him off across the road and on up a small side road. By the time he allowed them to ease the pace, Tony was so breathless he could barely speak above asking what had caused Steve's rough reaction,

"I was only asking politely to use her phone. And anyway, where the hell were you? If you hadn't gone off and left me on my own that wouldn't have happened! How was I supposed to know what to do or where to go?"

Trying hard to hold his temper, Steve turned and looked him in the eye and practically bellowed in his face,

"You're supposed to do like any other homeless, rough sleeper; find a way to survive without getting yourself arrested! Surely you don't really think, looking the way you do right now, that you can just walk up to a total stranger, especially a young woman, and expect her to hand over her phone or anything else to you. Even worse, you catch her just coming from a bank! You can think yourself lucky there were no coppers about or you'd be banged up by now."

Tony was clearly put out about being scolded like a kid. He wished he had the courage to argue the point with Steve, but could tell he stood no chance of winning if he did. He could see Steve had right on his side, so he'd clearly be the loser in that argument. Instead he fell back on what he saw as his best line of defence,

"So where were you then while I was getting it all wrong?"

The animosity in his voice was not lost on Steve who could tell that this meant that he was now realising that there were so many more problems connected to this lifestyle than he'd known about, or at least admitted to. Trying not to sound too self-satisfied, Steve briefly explained that he'd not been far away, and had been watching Tony from a distance to allow him to try going it alone for a while.

"Didn't go that well though did it?"

Feeling somewhat disgruntled by this answer, Tony was quick to say that he didn't reckon Steve should have done that without giving him warning of some sort, but as Steve quite rightly said, what would be the good of doing that? And anyway, the plan for the day was to separate for a few hours. He could see the struggle Tony was having to hide the panic he felt at that thought! Perhaps he'd now understood the lesson he'd just learnt about being cautious when approaching strangers. Perhaps he could get through a few hours alone if he kept himself to himself. He really would love to prove he wasn't as stupid as Steve was trying to make him look! He knew that to do that he would need to prove himself up to whatever he had to do to show himself capable of whatever he had to face that day.

They walked on some way from the town centre, almost in silence, before Steve stopped. He had already taken his hidden mobile from his bag, leaving it empty except the groundsheet they'd used before, Tony's old sleeping bag and a bottle of water. Passing the bag to Tony, Steve told him,

"Now, I'm going off for a while and it's up to you to sort out how to look after yourself and find something to eat. About ten miles that way," he says, pointing away from town, "there's a sort of commune, you know ... a sort of group of other homeless folks. I want you to go and persuade them to let you join them. I'll be along later," adding as an afterthought, "and try not to rub them up the wrong way or you'll be sleeping on the streets tonight!"

And to Tony's horror, he walked away.

Trying to muster all the strength and self-confidence he could, he set off in the direction Steve had indicated. Why, he wondered, had he ever allowed himself to be talked into all this in the first place? Why the hell had he agreed to accept the challenge for something he could now see he'd really never properly understood? But then, how was he ever going to come out of this without showing himself up? He had no answer to any of these questions.

As he came toward the edge of town it occurred to him that perhaps he should try to find some sort of food if he was to have a long walk ahead of him. From what Steve had said too, he would perhaps have to be prepared to have a contribution to offer these other 'tramps', as he still thought of them! All he hoped was that he'd be safe with them without Steve to keep them at a safe distance. After all, how did he know what they were like?

Reluctantly he lowered his dignity sufficiently as he passed the odd shops to politely ask if they had any 'out-of-date' food they'd consider letting him have, even offering to do any odd jobs they may have in return! Much to his surprise and relief, though he was reluctant to ask, the bakers gave him the job of sweeping the pavement outside and washing down the sills, in exchange for two loaves, both a little stale, though not quite to the point of being green, left from the previous day. He felt the baker was watching to see his reaction to this, so decided it best to say thank you and leave.

A little further along he was given the task of stacking boxes in the back yard of the greengrocers. They were just being delivered, and so held plenty of fresh fruit and veg but, to his disappointment and great annoyance, when he finished his task and was hoping to be given some of their contents, the shopkeeper came out and handed him a bag of assorted fruit and veg, most of which was well on the turn! As he walked away up the road he thought, what he could have done was to slip a few pieces of the fresh stuff into his bag while he was stacking them, but then he'd noticed one chap watching him from inside, so perhaps they'd not felt they could trust him!

Not for one minute did it occur to him that the men he'd noticed watching him at both shops, though dressed slightly differently from before, were the same two he'd already encountered. One of these dressed as the baker's assistant was in fact the same rather snobby chap who'd given him money to buy coffee rather than alcohol. The one at the greengrocers was actually the 'drug dealer' from outside the toilets! What he didn't know was that Steve had arranged this to collect proof of just what Tony had to do to get through his time alone.

He'd just set off out along the more open road away from town when the rain started to fall. At first this was only a light shower, but then built up to a good downpour. Not having much by way of a coat to keep him dry, Tony resorted to fishing out the groundsheet from the bag and wrapping it round himself. This worked reasonably well until, as he was trying to hitch a lift, a large lorry rushed by as he was passing a particularly deep puddle, and he found himself drenched from head to foot! He wouldn't have felt quite so bad about this had he not been convinced the driver swerved deliberately to do this, and seemed to be getting a good laugh at Tony's expense as he drove away.

Damn! That was the last straw, he thought. To make things worse, if that was possible, just after that, a car slowed in answer to his attempt to hitch a lift, but when the driver came close enough to see how bedraggled Tony was, he changed his mind and sped off, leaving him no choice but to find what shelter he could under the sparse trees around a layby. When the rain eased off he braved it and started out once more. Eventually, but not until he'd walked far enough to have dried off a bit, he was lucky enough to scrounge a lift in a delivery van. He told the driver he was looking for a group of people he'd been told were camping near here, and it seemed this wasn't so far. A way up the road, the van driver pulled up for him to climb out.

"Think you'll find the folk you're looking for in the woods over there," pointing across the road, "Good luck mate, they look a real motley crew to me!"

Of course, this didn't exactly fill Tony with confidence! But then, this is where Steve said he should go, and it was here Steve said he'd meet him later, so he really had no choice!

Chapter-Twenty-Five

With great trepidation Tony steeled himself to head toward the smell of wood burning which was drifting toward him. Reluctant as he was to approach a bunch of total strangers, the knowledge that they had a fire, and therefore hopefully hot food encouraged him forward. All he had to do was to keep them sweet and hope they just might share a little of whatever they have. He knew he had a few bits of food in his bag from the two shops he'd found work at, but he was well aware it wasn't particularly good quality. Dare he even offer it he wondered?

It was at this point that a noise coming from his left startled him, making him trip over a tree root he'd not noticed.

"Hello; who are you? What do you want here mate?"

Had it not been for the last word, 'mate', it was possible Tony would have panicked, but that alone made him think perhaps he should at least speak to this person. Mustering all the confidence he could, he turned to face the man who was by this time, standing over him. Much to his surprise though, he saw the hand being held out to help him up from where he'd fallen, and gratefully accepted it.

"Well, to be honest I'm just looking for a place to spend a night; and besides, someone told me to come in this direction and watch out for a group like yours. Said he'd meet me here eventually."

"Oh right, you must be Steve's mate then eh?"

Well, he thought, he wouldn't have thought of himself as being Steve's 'mate', but at least it seemed he'd found the right place, and they obviously knew Steve well enough to let him join them for now.

"I'm Ed. Come on and I'll introduce you to the others; Bill isn't it?"

Unsure whether he should make himself known by his real name he chose to go along with this. After all, he knew he must look anything but the smart TV presenter he really was. Ed took him a way further into the woods and closer toward the smoke that had attracted him in the first place. When the fire came into view, so did quite a gathering of people; men, women and even three or four children! Tony's first instinct was to want to ask just why anyone in their right mind would bring kids along to live a sort of gypsy lifestyle. But over this time he'd been living 'wild' himself, he felt it not his place to criticise.

Ed introduced him around the group, and much to his surprise it was not long before one of the women sat him by the fire with a hot drink. He noticed she had a pot hanging over the fire, and there was a smell of cooking drifting passed his nose. This was when he remembered the food in his bag.

"I've got a few vegetables in here, and a loaf; but none of them are very special I'm afraid. Thought they might have given me some decent stuff, but afraid all I was given was the rubbish, I'm sorry about that."

"Don't you worry about that, I can cut out the worst bits and then it'll all add to what's there already. When there's so many to feed, every little helps you know."

"My name is Bill by the way," he introduced himself to this woman.

She looked up from her task of chopping veg and removing bad bits, smiled sweetly, and introduced herself,

"Good to meet you Bill; my name's Mia."

Eventually most of the others introduced themselves, but of course, though to anyone not having visited Lansdown Grange, it would not have occurred that at least three were trusted residents of Steve's. Tony had to admit to himself just how accepting of him they all were. The one exception was a middle aged chap who chose to sit away from the fire, and therefore away from the main group. Tony hadn't noticed him until Mia served a couple of ladles of food onto a tin plate and took it to him. He had the urge to ask about the chap, but decided best to keep himself to himself (especially while there was hot food being dished out!). He did tentatively ask Ed how he knew Steve, but was just told that he'd called by the previous day and asked that they would look out for him and let him stay there until he came back!

They sat around the fire eating, Tony had to admit to himself that this stew made of practically anything that was going, including his half rotten vegetables, really was pretty good and nourishing, especially after the sort of day he'd had! It also gave him the opportunity to listen to the general conversations passing between them. He learnt how the couple with the two children had only come to live this way due to them having their house repossessed. The man had needed to give up full time work after his wife had developed cancer and died. The woman Tony had assumed was his wife, was actually his sister. She had given up her job to look after the children, but he was still not able to keep up the mortgage payments.

There was another couple in a similar position. It seems their home was rented, but still redundancy had seen them out on the streets. As they told Tony, yes it was true the councils should help find accommodation, but this was often substandard, and only temporary. One couple had been moved from one place to another so often, it had completely made it impossible for their kids to stay at one school for long enough to settle in. It seemed that Ed had once served a short term in jail for robbery after being led astray in his teens, but now at the age of about thirty was still finding no one willing to give him a chance at any meaningful long term work. It seemed from what Tony could find out about the couple who appeared to be in their late fifties, that they had been made homeless when their smallholding was compulsorily purchased for a new road to be built. When he asked why they'd not tried to start again somewhere else, they explained that the value which had been put on the land was insufficient to cover anything else at the time.

Tony was beginning to see that perhaps there were sometimes genuine reasons for these folk to be living rough after all. He was still curious about the odd chap sitting alone away from the fire though. Mia noticed this and came to sit by him. Before he thought to stop himself, Tony found himself asking her if this chap was on drugs? After all, he thought, why else would he be acting the way he was?

"Take no notice of Doug, he's just a bit of a wreck ... can't bare sitting too near the fire, but he's harmless really," and reading his mind, adding, "And no, he's not on drugs."

It was about then that a familiar voice came through the trees,

"Hope you've saved some of that for me. I'm starving!"

Tony looked round and saw Steve coming toward them through the trees. He couldn't help feeling pretty relieved though he wouldn't have admitted it. He'd begun to wonder if he would actually come, and if not, then what would he do?

"Hi Steve, pull up a log, you're just in time for a bite to eat before this greedy crew polish it off," said Mia with a grin.

At this point it appeared obvious to Tony that Mia, for one, seemed to be familiar with Steve. Perhaps the whole thing had been a set up all along? Perhaps none of what he'd experienced had been real, in which case this Lockett fellow was nothing more than a fraud, and a pretty rough one at that! After the way he'd dealt with those two ruffians who'd attacked him. And then again there was the way he'd laid into that pimp, if pimp he was?

Yet he had seemed to be a much calmer fellow in the way he'd apparently managed to work his way into the squat that night, but then he had never explained where the girl had gone. For all that Tony couldn't deny that Steve had quite probably saved him the embarrassment of getting arrested when he scared that woman outside the bank; clearly she wasn't in on any put up tricks of Lockett's! But then how about the rest of these people gathered around this fire?

He watched them carefully as they sat together chatting, but as much as he would have loved to catch him out, other than Mia and just possibly one couple, there were no obvious clues to go along with this theory. In fact it did seem that they were just happy to accept Steve in the same way they had him. At one point he noticed Mia whispering something to

Steve, presumably about Doug as they both looked across in his direction. Tony had noticed Doug had moved a little closer to gain warmth from the fire not long before this, but still stayed at a distance.

Steve looked casually in his direction and said in a quiet, reassuring voice,

"Come on man. It's warmer over here, and there's enough in that pot for you and me to share before these gannets get it all!"

As Tony watched, a rather hesitant and nervous Doug began to approach the log Steve was sitting on. But then something totally unexpected happened. Two of the young boys arrived back from collecting more firewood and threw a large bundle straight onto the fire, causing it, due to being slightly damp, to set off a sudden crashing noise as it landed, followed by a sudden explosion of loud crackling and hissing. To Tony's amazement he saw Doug throw himself on the ground, hands over his ears, shaking like a leaf, and crying like a baby!

Tony had never seen such a reaction from anyone. All he could do was sit with a horrified expression watching, while Steve leapt straight into action! He was off the log and over to Doug in an instant.

"It's ok soldier. It's nothing to worry about mate; just the damp wood on the fire crackling. You're quite safe ... you have my word on it."

Doug felt Steve's hand on his back and heard the calming voice. Steve was kneeling by his side and clearly seemed to understand what was going on. Tony would like to have gone across to find out what the problem was but Mia put her hand out to prevent him doing so.

"No," She told him firmly, "Keep away. Leave it to Steve, he knows what to do. Should do by now after all."

"What do you mean? What's the matter with the man? And what makes Lockett qualified to deal with him more than anyone else?"

For a second or two Mia looked at him in sheer disbelief before realising that he truly was ignorant of the situation!

"Poor chap's ex-army. He's got a bad case of PTSD. None of us," she looked around at the others, "have been able to do a thing with him when something sets him off like that."

"Ok, so why Lockett?"

Mia sighed heavily before explaining,

"You really are ignorant when it comes to him aren't you man? Steve was an ex-paratrooper. Had a hell of a long, awful couple of tours in Afghanistan. Then when they sent him home to recover from PTSD, his wife, kid and sister were all killed together in a car crash on the way to pick him up!"

"Bloody hell! No I didn't know that. Did he get help with it?"

"No. Seems he couldn't face it. Just went walk-about and lived rough for a couple of years till he met Mel. I reckon she's the best thing that ever happened to him. It was thanks to her he accepted help. Since they've been together he's completely rebuilt his life."

And then, more to herself than to Tony, she added warmly,

"And now he's dedicated his life to helping dozens of others do exactly the same."

Chapter Twenty-Six

Back at the Grange I was pleased to see the way our Will had stepped up to take his father's place. Lilly, in spite of her somewhat cumbersome proportions, split her days between helping me with the endless administration work, and taking time most afternoons to keep May company.

Though I was aware of her health becoming increasingly weakened, I was so glad to see how much May had truly immersed herself in her family, and had at last been able to look on Lansdown as Steve's rightful home, and no longer had any black thoughts of what had happened to her here so many years ago. Even so, my concern was growing for Steve to come home as I felt in some ways that she was missing him, if possible, even more than I was!

Since Steve and Tony had left, our numbers had increased by a couple. It seems that one fellow had been given a card by a chap he'd met and told to make his way here and ask for Mel! Apparently he'd been living rough for some time and quite expected to be turned away, but thought it worth a try. We couldn't really say no after all now, could we?

When Chris took a small group from here to help Steve, much to our surprise he had come back with a young lady by the name of Sarah. Poor kid was a bit of a wreck. She'd been under the control of a pimp who had got her hooked on drugs to make use of her to earn money. From what Chris told us, Steve sorted him out in no uncertain manner (as I would expect of him of course!), and sent her back here for full rehabilitation, and a place of safety. It took a few days sticking close to me before I could persuade her she was now safe. We were lucky to have a really good female doctor in the village who was happy to come here to check her out and work with her to begin the gradual process of weaning her from the drugs.

Chris decided that it wasn't worth driving back to his place straight away, and so stayed to help Will with running Steve's exercise regime amongst the residents! There was also another little job Steve had set him and Will to do. The main hall had to be set up as a studio, and with the inside help from the TV people, prepared to show footage of their expedition, allowing seating for Tony, Steve and those involved, plus seating for an audience of press etc. As Steve had told me that day after we'd been to the TV studio, he wouldn't stand for people tarring all rough sleepers and homeless folks as dirty scroungers! They need to listen to what puts people in that position ... not to judge something they don't understand!

It was clear that the ever-present swarm of press outside our walls were not giving up. If anything their numbers were increasing. They had more or less set up a permanent encampment outside in the hope of being first in line to film the return of our two wanderers, making it almost impossible to leave without sneaking out under cover of darkness! On the whole we didn't allow this to hinder our work so much.

But then, two days after Chris and Sarah arrived back here, there was an almighty storm one night! We were lucky in as much as it barely affected the Grange except for taking down one tree and branches from a few more, but then news came through to us via one of our chaps who Steve had found work for with a building firm in the village, that he'd been unable to reach there. It seemed that the roads both in and out of the village were completely blocked by fallen trees, one end being so blocked as to form a complete dam across the river! He came back to ask for us to send help as this was now rising so fast that a row of cottages one end were already flooded inside, and more were under serious threat of joining them. The locals had tried calling for help, but the power was off and phone lines had come down with the trees.

This was without a doubt, the first time I could honestly say just how amazed and proud I truly was of Will. Now I could honestly see just how much like his father he was! Without hesitation, and with such command, he rallied as many able-bodied men, women and equipment, and with Chris along to back him up, all set off to do what they could for the villagers, taking little notice of the excited trail of press, hungry to see where they were heading. According to Chris, our Will even managed to shame some of these to put down their cameras and lend a hand!

Under Will and Chris's supervision they worked non-stop, many up to their shoulders cutting up the dams which had formed, and passing it from hand to hand until it finally released the rush of water which had been causing such devastation!

Of course, with our bunch of TV groupies always ready to follow anyone leaving the Grange, much of this was filmed and shown live on the local news. It was then that May, Lilly and myself saw something truly amazing. It seemed that one young boy of about seven years old had found himself on the wrong side of the water, and had tried to climb across one of the fallen trees. This just may have worked had it not been for a fresh gush of water from upstream hitting the tree, sending him falling in and disappearing from view! On the TV we watched, horrified, as his mother stood on the bank screaming.

Within seconds we saw Will rush along the bank, dive straight in, so reminiscent of the time his father had dived in to save me from the dam all those years back, and a second later pop back up with the lad firmly in his grasp! Chris rushed across, took him from Will and handed him into his mother's arms, before holding out a hand to Will and rewarding him with a good firm pat on the back. I couldn't help hearing him say,

"Quick thinking young Lockett. No prizes for guessing who your father is eh?"

The news that evening was full of on-the-spot filming of the whole event! As our residents finished the major work or clearing the debris so that the authorities could get in to take over, the villages came out in force, plying them with hot drinks and the odd tot of whisky to ward off the chill, and without exception, even those who would before have had a low opinion of having a rabble like them on their doorstep, could not speak more highly of them to the watching press.

What Will and our residents achieved that day was to bring about a whole new view of the work of Lansdown Grange, just by a stroke of luck, shown across the country by the very media we had spent days trying to hide away from!

Chapter Twenty-Seven

Two days after this event, and with no knowledge of what had been taking place here, Steve rang to ask for Chris to go to pick him up. It seemed he needed him to take our mini-bus this time as, along with him and Tony, there was also of course Bob, Ellen and Mia, but he was bringing with them an extra chap by the name of Doug. Of course we knew nothing about this chap, except for the fact that Steve had specially requested Paul, our ex-army counsellor, to be brought along. This didn't bode well. It told me straight away that this was undoubtedly some poor chap suffering PTSD as I'd seen Steve struggle with so long ago.

In fact, even to this day, and quite probably for the rest of his days, I know he'll never be completely free of it. There are still days when I can sense it creeping over him like a dense black mist, and I know that on those days there's not a thing I, or anyone else, can do but to leave him to take himself off alone with his thoughts and wait … wait and pray that the mist will eventually lift and he will come home. The main saving grace in all of this was that word, 'home'. In Steve's case it did take an awful long time and the experienced counselling of Paul before he was even considered to be recovered enough to be safe out in public. It was a very gradual process, not helped by him having spent so long alone, running away from his own conscience brought about by a misplaced feeling of guilt.

Even as he was on that road to recovery he couldn't seem to completely shake off this need to keep on the move, almost as if he was still looking for something or somewhere. Perhaps he was; perhaps he was still (as May had said) following his rainbow in search of his hopes and dreams. Now he had truly accepted Lansdown Grange as his home, he was a new, much more contented man.

And now he was bringing home another poor soul in the condition he knew only too well. I knew that, with Paul's help, this would be giving this chap the best chance possible. With this in mind I set too preparing a quiet, private room, close to Paul's quarters. All I hoped was that we could give him the support and comfort he needed to recover as best he could. Of course, he'd not been the first ex-serviceman we've taken in under Paul's care, but somehow I knew that this new one must be one of the worst cases or Steve wouldn't have made the decision to come home nearly five days earlier than planned.

Knowing they were coming that day meant that everyone here at the Grange had to set to and be sure that everything was just as Will had requested. Nobody here had been made to take part in his planned televising of what he had in mind though. In fact it had been almost as Steve had left home that, without either his or Tony's knowledge, but with the complete agreement of the programme planners, that Will had enlisted the help and cooperation of at least eighty per cent of the residents to see to it that the time and effort Steve had put into this had not gone to waste.

All those willing to take part by being interviewed by the reporters made special efforts to see to it that their quarters, whether it be in the dormitories, or in the assorted pods and odd small bungalows scattered about the vast grounds, were immaculate! They were keen to prove that, with the help and encouragement of our family and staff, it was possible to turn around the lives they'd struggled with before, and to become useful and respectable members of society. In fact, it wasn't until I opened the office door one morning expecting to have a few come forward to put their names on the list to take part, that I fully understood myself just how much our work meant to so many! I was greeted by a queue stretching along the landing, down the stairs, and out onto the front terrace.

Of the few choosing to remain unseen, these were mostly the ones who'd not been here long enough to feel properly secure, or in a couple of cases, not wishing those who had perhaps abused them previously to know of their whereabouts. This was duly noted and they agreed to stay out of sight on the day.

It seemed that Josh had prepared a menu of good quality snacks (all finger food as we really didn't want them expecting a sit-down do), and had enlisted a small group to help him in the preparation and laying out on the day. All those he could muster as staff on that day he proudly turned out in immaculate white jackets. I couldn't help thinking that our dining room was going to look like that of a top hotel.

On the previous day, though without mentioning exactly when the wanderers were to return, Will went to the front gate to address the crowds camped outside. May and I had walked down with him, but chose to stay well back inside the gate and just observe with great pride just how well he handled them. Not for a minute did he allow them to fluster him, or push him for more information than he wanted to give them.

What he told them was that his father and Tony Maningly were returning soon. He went on to say that, when this happened, they were to stay back away from the gate to allow the vehicle to enter. Only then would a number of them be invited in to a press conference and chance to be shown around the estate to see just what our work here entailed. Of course they pushed forward and shouted questions at Will, but he never once wavered from his prepared speech.

"Oh dear Mel, you must feel so very proud of your boy," May remarked, "Watching the way he's taken command of that bunch reminds me so much of his father. Steve was always like that ... even in the way he took control of his younger brothers after Peter passed away."

As we walked back up away from the closed gate Will whispered quietly to us that he thought he'd said enough to throw them off the scent by making it pretty obvious that they would be coming straight in through the front gate in the mini-bus with Chris driving.

Meanwhile he had told Paul to send a warning message to one of the men he would place near the small rear gate so that they were ready for Steve to drive in through this gate in Chris's van. He'd told Steve these would be a few of our chaps just happening to work near that entrance, and as soon as they saw the van approach they were to open the gate for just long enough for the van to come in, before closing it quickly! Hopefully any still there would assume that this was some sort of tradesman's van and not recognise Steve. After all, as he told us, by now Steve would look well scruffy!

The scene was set, all we needed now were the players!

Chapter Twenty-Eight

Having everything set up so efficiently meant that we could all spend that night feeling relaxed and, certainly in my case, more than a little excited about what was to happen tomorrow. I could feel the relief flowing from May with the knowledge that her boy was coming home where he belonged (there's that word, 'home' again!), and of course for me the thought that by tomorrow night I would no longer be in that big, empty bed alone. Over the time he'd been away, though not so very long on the face of it, I'd realised just how much I'd come to think of the real 'home' for me was laying, wrapped in those strong arms of his, usually following the thrill of him releasing his almost animal passion on me! From that first time by the lake after he'd saved me from drowning, we had been totally committed to each other, as the wedding vows say, to the exclusion of all others.

So there we sat together, May just longing to see her boy safely home, Will wanting (or hoping), to seek his father's approval, Lilly just pleased for Will and looking forward to see her parents, and me … well, I'll leave that to your imagination!

As we sat together having a drink and a slice of May's homemade fruit cake later on we switched on the TV and watched with amusement as the reporters on both main channels excitedly showed film of Will, outside the gate, and their attempts to drag more information from him but to no avail.

"But don't worry viewers, when this happens we'll be here to catch everything so there'll be no need to miss the excitement. We can be sure this will be in a couple of days from now, so keep tuning in."

Will cracked up laughing at the way he'd deceived them into thinking there were still a few days to go! As he said, if they'd caught on to the fact that Steve would be here tomorrow, they'd probably be swarming all over like ants!

"Can't wait to see how it went, and how much they managed to get on film. I wonder if Dad has managed to get through to that self-opinionated fool. You can bet he'll do his best to deny everything and try to make Dad look small."

"Don't worry on that score Will. I think your Dad will have got the upper hand of him by now. I've seen him do that with far worse men than him, and enjoyed doing so at that."

In fact, what so many people chose not to take into account when confronted by the homeless in society, is a point of view which Steve had learnt to take into account right back before we met. From choosing to live rough himself he learnt over some time that there were many varied reasons for folk being on the streets. Ok, he had chosen to go it alone (but then he did have quite a heavy burden to deal with, one he wrongly believed he needed to cope with that way), but whilst he was out there, experiencing it first hand as it were, he came into contact with so many with every imaginable reason for living that way.

Some had been made homeless due to financial problems, some (especially the youngsters) had found themselves in abusive relationships and had deliberately chosen to live on the streets rather than continue being abused.

Of course, and Steve has never denied this, there are what you might call, 'the bad apples' in this barrel, those who find it easier to hang around in doorways begging for hand-outs, and then going off to spend what they get in pubs or on drugs, with no intention of attempting to live better lives, or to work for a living. These are the ones who give the less fortunate such a bad reputation, and therefore make it harder for the genuinely needy to find help.

Having watched the ten o'clock news, finished our drinks and sat chatting for a while I could see that May was looking particularly tired, in fact I'd been aware for some time now that she was beginning to tire much quicker lately. I suggested it was time to turn in for the night as it sounded like being a busy day the next day. Lilly was quick to see my mind and all but pushed Will out to take her home to their bungalow.

"Come on Will. I think this little one," patting her bulge, "Is wanting sleep, and so do I."

Looking hesitant at first, until I directed a quick glance at May to him to show what we both were thinking. He was quick to catch on to our meaning, and so gave out a false yawn, gave her a goodnight kiss, and escorted Lilly home while I helped May up and made sure she was tucked up comfortably in her bed. Only then did I climb into mine, feeling like a kid at Christmas, knowing that Steve, like Santa, would be here tomorrow!

The next morning started early at Lansdown Grange. Determined to see that everything ran like clockwork, Will and I were up and out at the crack of dawn. I must say, we were surprised to find our residents were equally eager as those who always took part in our (usually Steve's) exercise group, were outside warming up as we walked out the door! In fact it was one of them who specially requested that our morning jog took a route along past the wall where it ran right by the camping out press tents and vehicles. I couldn't understand their reasoning at first as they usually preferred to avoid these folks, but then it became clear. As we passed their spot, our bunch 'decided' it was a good spot to stop for stretching exercises with Will shouting instructions like a sergeant major, and them yelling replies in equally loud voices! At first I did try to quieten them down, but then thought, why shouldn't I join in! They'd been there giving us so much hassle for so long, why not give them some back while we had the chance. It didn't take long before we heard complaining voices coming from their encampment, so at that point we decided we'd got our own back, so moved on before they had chance to work out just what had caused the disturbance.

By the time we returned to the Grange there was just time for the less active amongst our folk to join us on the front lawn for a session of gentle stretching and light exercise to whatever level they felt appropriate. We, or should I say Steve, still insisted that everyone should attempt some form of fitness work out unless medically unable to do so. I must admit to thinking that perhaps he was being rather fanatical about this back when we first set up this place, but now so long after, I have to admit that his theory that a healthy body leads to a healthy mind has been proved so many times. I've seen youngsters with no self-pride, those attempting to wean themselves off of drugs or drink, or just those with no hope of rebuilding their lives, all gradually turn the corner to become better people, helped in great part by being pushed into becoming fitter than they believed possible.

By the time we had all gone off to shower, dress and check that everywhere was ready for scrutiny, all were more than ready to face whatever the day was to bring, and all, without exception, determined to do whatever it took to show just how much Lansdown Grange, and in particular Steve, meant to them all.

All that was left now was to enjoy the hearty breakfast prepared for them and wait.

Chapter Twenty-Nine

Having helped Josh and his helpers (or should I say, 'waiters') complete the job of turning the dining room from that of general use, to the look of the highest quality restaurant, I returned back upstairs to check on May. Quite expecting her to choose to stay safely tucked away from the events due to unfold later, I was surprised to find her already changed into her best outfit, sitting regally in the armchair near the window, obviously in the hope of seeing her son return!

"What time do we expect him dear?" she asked.

It seemed she had absolutely no intention of missing the fun. I had to explain that we really had no exact time, but thought it wouldn't be too long. It would have been difficult at that time to say which one of us was more eager to see him walk in the door. All I could assure her was that they were definitely on their way, but from where, we had no idea? The truth being that he had told nobody where they had gone. The only way Chris had found him the time he'd brought Sarah back, and again now that he'd gone to pick them up, was by using the tracker Steve had on his mobile, and until Chris received a signal from him, even he had no idea! It was yet another example of the ex-para training shared by them both ... never make your location obvious!

An hour later Lilly came to tell us that Will and a few men had gone to the gate. It seems they were inviting in the producers of Tony's show, plus representatives from an assortment of other media. He made it clear to the rest that, once he knew how much room was left, a number of them may also be let in, but only as long as they followed strict guidelines. No hassling of those returning, or attempts to roam unescorted, would be tolerated. I think having a few of our largest and toughest men along to back him up seemed to convince them to cooperate. After all, as far as they knew, these were made up of vagrants, druggies and the like! They were not prepared to risk their safety for a scrap of news which could be worthless, whatever their bosses might have told them.

By ten thirty I had helped May to take a seat on the edge of the stage. I really was rather worried about her attending this event at all to be honest. After all, although I had in the past explained to her just what Steve had looked like when I met him living rough, I was worried that the shock of actually seeing this herself may be too much, but she was adamant that we should show a united front against any doubters. I couldn't help thinking just what a wonderful mother this lady was.

A few minutes later there was a steady stream of press folk pouring in, most with microphones but the main channels spent a while setting up cameras, microphones, lights etc. It was left to our plumber, Dave, and a group he had organised, to see to it that they all found seats and behaved in an orderly fashion as soon as possible. May, Lilly and myself were under strict orders not to speak to anyone until Will came back to speak to them first.

Unfortunately that meant we weren't in a position to see the fun unfolding outside, but all was revealed to us later!

Everything out there apparently was running like a military operation. Between Steve and Chris, and of course Will, it seemed that what was happening was this.

The minute Steve gave a signal through to Chris and Will, Will put the workers at the back gate on stand-by to watch for the van approaching. Then, simultaneously, both gates would be open briefly. By this time the press at the front would have seen the mini-bus approaching and called those at the rear. These would rush to the front, not wishing to miss it.

The folk in the bus would keep their heads down so they'd not be recognised, while the important folk, Steve, Tony, Doug and Paul, would sneak in at the back! This would give Paul the opportunity to whisk away Doug to the quiet, private rooms he'd prepared for him next to his own, so that he wouldn't be disturbed.

Imagine the looks of surprise and disappointment on the faces of the waiting press outside to find that the bus, instead of bringing Steve and Tony, other than Chris driving actually only brought Bob, Ellen, Mia plus the two men who'd played the parts of the 'posh chap' (who'd offered Tony money for coffee instead of booze), and the make-believe drug dealer!

Good as his word, Will then allowed in as many more press as there was room for, before locking the gates and leaving a couple of men standing guard at each. Once the hall was full to capacity he went through to the back door and opened it, allowing Steve and Tony in and straight onto the stage (much to Steve's reluctance). The whole place appeared to erupt in applause, but Steve ignored this and walked straight up to May first, and then me, giving us both a good firm hug! I watched May's face carefully as he came in, quite expecting her to be shocked, but I was glad to see that, if she was, she managed to hide it well. As for myself, I had all I could do to let go of him ... but still found myself getting a laugh from seeing the old, wild Steve once more!

For a few hectic minutes they were bombarded with questions and dazzled with flash lights from all corners of the hall, but Will spoke to them over a microphone, telling them to sit down and wait ... nobody on the stage was going to speak until there was order, and then he would invite a few questions, but only a very few, as 'Mr Lockett and Mr Maningly would then be allowed time to freshen up and change before the main interviews would be allowed'.

In fact the most they had time to do was to take enough photos to show, as you might say, the before and after effect of their expedition. As soon as they started throwing questions about where they'd been and how Tony had coped, Will, with a bit of help from the firm hand and dominating figure of Chris in the hall doorway, ushered the two men out and up to our quarters. I whispered in Steve's ear that I had already laid out the clean clothes and shaving gear the studio people had given us for Tony and provided him with clean towels, and that he should point Tony to our shower, and that I'd laid out all of his clean things in May's room for him to use her shower.

"Ok, thanks my love,"

But just as he turned to go he turned back to me and whispered,

"How about coming to scrub my back though? I reckon I could use some help after what I've been through, and there's room for two after all."

If we hadn't been in a room full of strangers, to say nothing of his mother, I would have given him a rude answer

... or perhaps even taken him up on the offer! As it was all I could do was glare at him (to supress the smile creeping up), and tell him to clear off and get clean!

As I went back to my chair Will came up to sit next to me. He threw me a worried look and asked,

"Are you feeling ok Mum? You look rather flushed."

What could I say? Especially when sat between him and May.

"Yes dear, I'm fine. It must just be the heat in here with so many people squashed in together. Perhaps I'll pop up and see Dad has all he needs. Give me chance to cool off."

As I passed Chris at the door I might have known he'd have something to say.

"You'll need to make it quick girl ... but I reckon he's good at that, eh?"

Chapter Thirty

By the time the three of us came back down to the hall all those in there had been served with drinks and were sitting down patiently (well, almost) waiting for us to reappear. Will had explained to them that this was just to tide them over until after the conference, and that following that there would be a buffet lunch served in the dining room, courtesy of our resident chef and staff. Chris was still standing guard at the hall door to stop anyone hoping to roam uninvited. As I passed him with Steve he couldn't resist a glance at his watch, a wink, and whispering,

"Not too bad for his age"

Well, of course that had the effect of making me look even more flushed than before! So much so that Will once again asked if I was sure I was ok. He even went as far as to say to Steve that he was a little worried about me, and that perhaps he should see I had an early night tonight! Little did he know, that was just what Steve had in mind, but not for the same reason!

As soon as we were all seated Will announced to the press that he was first going to show some footage of the time Tony had been away, with Steve giving a commentary. He would then hand over to Tony to pass his comments on how it went. Only then would questions be taken.

We moved temporarily to one side, revealing a large screen on the back wall, and watched as the film taken by

Steve's secret cameras was revealed. Tony was clearly extremely put out about this, as he was quick to point out when the end came, he'd not been consulted about it. And anyway, he asked, just who had taken it, and why couldn't he have had his people do it?

Steve was quick to explain that he wanted a true picture rather than one that had been fixed to make Tony look good. What Tony hadn't known at the time was that parts of his journey had been taken from small cameras attached to Chris at the very beginning, then Bob and on occasions to Ellen, all from a safe distance without being seen. In fact there were two occasions when Bob had played visible parts. One of these was dressed as the posh bloke who'd thrown coins at him! And then again, after a change of clothes, as the drug dealer outside the toilets! Even then, when Tony had finally reached the camp at the end, he still didn't recognise Bob as someone he'd met earlier! In fact he had to admit, the only face he did recognise now was Mia. As he realised when she appeared a few minutes ago, this was the kind young lady who had been happy to feed him … a total stranger.

Following this it was Will who took control of those wanting to throw questions at Tony and Steve. I couldn't help thinking just how well he kept control of the proceedings, allowing it to be done in a controlled fashion. One after another they asked all manner of things. Whose idea had it been that Tony should set off dressed that way? How much money did he take with him? When Tony assured them that it had been down to Steve on both counts, they turned the question on Steve.

"Well, your man here wanted the true experience of being homeless, and that's what I gave him. We weren't out there for fun you know. That's the whole point ... there is no fun in being homeless!"

"Well, what did you do for food then," one chap asked.

"You ask your fellow here. He soon learnt the hard way that you have to be grateful for any scraps anyone cares to dish out."

"Even if it's stale bread and mouldy cheese!" Tony chipped in.

There was a noticeable 'yuck' sound from amongst the press. They clearly assumed that Tony would only be looking on from the side-lines, as it were. Not actually getting right deep into this experience! One chap did actually put forward the relevant question of why there were so many homeless, when there were empty houses in certain parts of the country.

At this point, and just as I could see an exasperated Steve was about to get up and tell them to 'f off' if they were not prepared to use their brains, to the great surprise of all on the stage, Tony stood up and walked forward to take a microphone from the crew. I wondered what was going to happen now. Should I signal for Chris to come over and remove Steve before he exploded?

Before I had time to do so Tony was addressing his audience.

"Now just listen to me and I'll see you're given a clear picture and details of anything you need to know. To your first question of why are so many homeless, the first lesson I learnt during this time was this. It's a never-ending circle of no work, no rent money, no rent, no home. I was put in the situation of seeking employment, and was actually offered some until they found I had, in the guise of a character named 'Bill', no permanent address. Officially we all need an address to be employed. At that point I felt the humiliation of being turned away. Having never been out of work for a day in my life I can tell you, this came as a real blow."

The audience mumbled amongst themselves, obviously not expecting their man to be on the side of these he'd previously called 'dregs of society'! To our surprise, in particular Steve's, he more or less took over the biggest part of the interview, answering the most difficult questions which had obviously been prepared to take his side and show Steve up, but Tony was having none of it!

He went over the whole experience, clearly happy to show his change of attitude on the whole subject. There were murmurings across the room. Someone stood up and asked him,

"Didn't you feel you might be in danger at any time Mr Maningly? I mean, were you ever threatened by anyone?"

With a quick glance behind him at Steve, he turned back to his audience with something of a grin on his face.

"Yes, I did feel in danger on a couple of occasions … on one of them I was actually attacked by a couple of thugs; but I was under the protection of one of the most capable and trustworthy men I've ever had the privilege to know, Steve Lockett!"

"So were these homeless, the ones who attacked you?"

Tony assured them they were not.

"Just how did Mr Lockett protect you?"

With another glance in Steve's direction for permission as it were, he went on to say,

"Wish that bit was on film, but the way he handled two of them at once was, believe me, a sight to behold. All I can say is, I'd suggest you don't upset him!"

Chris and I did our best not to laugh, having seen him in action on many occasions. Will and May looked across at him with pride, and in May's case, a little curiosity.

"Ok, so when else did you feel in danger?"

Tony explained to them about the time he made the mistake of approaching the woman coming from the bank and Steve had leapt into action to remove him from harm's way. This caused some amusement.

He almost overstepped the line when he went on to tell them of how Steve had come to the aid of a young girl who had been hooked on drugs by a pimp. His audience were quick to pounce on this to ask just what happened then. I could see that Steve was about to get to his feet to stop Tony expanding on the incident, but before he had chance to do so, a quiet voice came from the door,

"He gave him a bloody good hiding and sent me here to be with Mel or I'd never have got away."

Everyone looked round to see this young girl who had just sneaked into the back of the hall unseen!

"Sarah no. You don't need to get involved in this," Steve said as he dashed across to rescue her from the press who had turned to see her and were about to bombard her mercilessly with questions.

"No, please, let me tell them what happens to the likes of me. They need to know to try to stop it happening to others ... and believe me, there's always more poor beggars just like I was."

With obvious reluctance, Steve walked her up to stand with him on the stage. Tony stood to one side, once again listening to the explanation Steve had given him back then about what happens to eighteen year olds in care. Having seen what a nervous wreck she'd been last time he'd seen her, Tony was amazed at just how determined she was to have her say to so many. He'd not given much thought to where she'd gone since he saw her at the squat. Back then he remembered thinking that there was no chance of her ever recovering from the life she'd been leading. Now he knew this was where Steve had sent her, and he was genuinely impressed at the change in her in such a short time. Whatever they do with these people here, he thought to himself, clearly works. In fact, in Sarah's case, it was nothing short of miraculous!

Of course, the questions flew fast and hard ... what had they done to her since she got here, was she treated kindly, was she locked up so that she couldn't go away?"

At this I found the need to get to my feet and have a say. I was quick to assure them that nobody here is ever locked up! What would be the point of that? If they want help to recover from anything, drink, drugs or abuse, it had to be of their own choosing. All we ever insisted on was that they abide by our rules, and don't think it's a holiday camp! Someone shouted from the floor to ask what happened if they didn't and were found flouting these rules.

"They go out that gate faster than you lot came in a while ago," Steve was quick to tell them.

This caused a fair reaction, mixed between laughter and disbelief. Will joined in at this minute. He came up to stand with his father and me. When the noise settled down he took charge once more to explain that he now intended to introduce a small group of our friends who would explain, from their point of view, just how the work at Lansdown had begun so long ago. Without warning Steve he had spoken with Dave, Graham, Pete and Bob, and they had been more than happy to come on stage in turn to explain how we'd all met that time long ago and, when Steve took over the place, had been more than willing to stay on for the purpose of helping many (in particular, youngsters) try their hand at the skills they were themselves qualified at.

Questions flew thick and fast, one in particular about the purpose of this. Steve was quick to explain that, with encouragement, if they had an interest in taking this further, he would do his best to help find them work, apprenticeships, or even college courses.

"So why couldn't they find work without your help then?" piped up one.

"If you'd listened to what your chap here told you, if they don't have a permanent address, they can't get work!"

There was silence for a brief second or two until one of them, thinking this was a joke, said,

"So they tell the employers their address is Lansdown Grange eh? Bit grand isn't it?"

"Maybe, but it obviously works or they'd never leave, and we'd be overflowing."

At this point Will took over once more, having organised the whole event, and called an end to this part of it. He explained to them all that it was now time for the buffet lunch prepared by Josh and his staff, during which time, on condition they acted in a civilised manner, they could feel free to speak to any residents there.

With a number of these acting as guides they could then be shown round to see the accommodation and meet more residents. They were, under no circumstances, to open any doors which were closed, as this could be quarters of newer folk not wishing to be seen for whatever reason and their privacy must be respected.

Just then, before I had chance to look round, I was suddenly aware of a man's voice behind me. I turned to see two of the reporters, one each side of poor May, throwing questions at her about Steve and how he'd come to inherit the house and where he got his money from! All I did catch of what she did say to them was that owning it had given him chance to follow a dream of his but, unlike following a rainbow, this one had no pot of gold at the end, which meant he probably wouldn't be able to keep it going. Before I had chance to take a step toward them to come to her rescue, to their amazement they found themselves grabbed by the collar by Steve, one in each hand, and marched out of the front door, down the drive, and literally thrown out of the gate, with Chris holding it open for him! The chap nearest me as I went to the door to watch this event, happened to be Tony's producer. He watched on in sheer disbelief, then turned to me to ask,

"Whatever made your husband do that?"

"Well," I told him, trying not to give way to the laughter I really felt just then, "Steve had warned them what happens to anyone who disobeys his rules. Never mind ... at least he put them out the gate, not over it!"

Chapter Thirty-One

It seems that news of Steve's actions spread quickly amongst our visitors that afternoon. Though it was pretty obvious that they would have dearly liked to poked around in all corners of the house and assorted accommodation, and were tempted to open the odd locked door in the hope of finding ... well, finding what? The skeletons in our cupboard perhaps! But we were lucky to have sufficient residents keen to help show these people how they had been helped by being given a place of safety to come to when their lives were drifting into the mire, and a chance to rebuild them.

Without interference or supervision from any of us in authority, they were allowed to see for themselves the accommodation, from the dormitories to the individual pods. They saw too the few small bungalows converted from the old outbuildings, and now used for couples.

Having seen May safely upstairs and left Josh on guard duty to see that nobody went up to our quarters, I went outside to join Steve and Chris. Steve had decided not to go round with the press as he reckoned it would make it look as if he had something to hide, but Will, Pete and Bob hovered around just close enough to keep a watchful eye on them.

It wasn't so long before Tony came back to speak to Steve, of course complete with cameraman and microphone and his producer. He'd seen the barn across behind the buildings, and was keen to ask what we used this for. Steve explained that we held weddings, conferences and the like when we were asked, in fact, as he said, we had been married in there ourselves, as had our son and his wife.

"We also hold local scout and cub camps in here when conditions outside aren't good enough," I piped up.

"So you must get on pretty well with the locals then, to let you bring their kids here amongst your ... your residents I mean?"

"Of course we do. If you'd been around last week when we had the storm that caused the river to break its bank, you'd know it was our 'residents' who stepped up to come to their rescue!"

I could see straight away that I'd hit a nerve with my remark, but at the same time I could see that it had the desired effect.

Just before Tony and his particular crew left, I invited them up to our quarters for tea or coffee, just to see they did actually leave with a good impression, and to let Tony put over to his camera a little of his thoughts on his adventures. Of course, when they eventually all left, we had no way to know exactly what impression any of us had made, or what the fall-out from all of this would be.

Steve had done what he set out to do and all of us back here had all done our best, but this could either work in our favour or against us. Who could tell? Lilly and Ellen had prepared a hot meal for us all, one which I could see went down particularly well with Steve! Though I know he's quite able to live on what could be called survival rations, I also know he's got just that little bit used to the easy life over the years! Over dinner he had chance to fill us all in on the events of his time away, giving us the amusing bits which he'd kept from the press. May turned in not long after this, and it wasn't long before Will, Lilly, Bob and Ellen took themselves away to bed too.

Though I loved our family dearly, this was what I'd been aching to do ... to be alone with my dear Steve. It always struck me just how much I hated being without him by my side, even for the shortest time. As I curled up on the sofa with his arm around me I could still feel, as I always did even after so many years, that same feeling of warmth, safety, and a deep love which had found its way into my heart from that first day when he'd taken me under his protection. I've never known why it had been me he'd chosen to allow into his heart after choosing to be alone for so long, but now I knew we were meant to be together.

We drank two more glasses of wine each to finish the bottle left from dinner, but otherwise just sat in comfortable silence. The television was on quietly in the corner of the room, but we were in no mood to watch it, our only interest right then was in one another's company and the gentle and loving kisses we shared. Steve got up to switch it off as the remote had been left on the chair Will had been on across the room. Just before he did so he hesitated, listening to an announcement,

"Tune in tomorrow morning for the Tony Maningly morning show to see footage of his time with the homeless of our society. Listen to the interview with him and Mr Steve Lockett. See the filming and interview with those from the Lockett's facility for the less fortunate, and form your own opinion of what goes on behind the walls of Lansdown Grange."

Steve switched it off before more could be said, and came back to sit by me. I said nothing ... I desperately didn't want our beautifully warm and loving feeling to be brushed aside by it. I needn't have worried on that score of course. I've known my Steve long enough to know that it takes more than that to put him off when he has his mind set on something, and right then I knew just what he had his mind fixed on!

Without another word, he pulled me to my feet, lifted me in his arms as if I was a child, and carried me to our bed. What happened after this was, of course, not in any way childlike! In fact, after just a couple of week's abstinence, I knew he would be almost desperate! Don't get me wrong mind you ... I was as eager as him, and I knew I wouldn't be disappointed, in all these years I never have been. What I've always been so amazed by though is, that in spite of his almost animal appetite, he's always been able to satisfy us both with such tenderness, never once forcing himself on me if I'm not wanting him, but why would I not?

Not another word was spoken that night, there was nothing else to say. As I cuddled up tightly in his arm, I wondered what the next day would bring forth ... but who cared? Just then we were where we belonged ... together.

Chapter Thirty-Two

The next morning before breakfast I suggested to Steve that he should leave Will dealing with the morning exercise group, but he insisted that he should go. It seems he'd missed this while he'd been away. As he opened the door I couldn't help a little giggle escaping from me at the shocked look on a few faces! I think Will, having done his best to work them, had not quite matched up to his father in that respect! Obviously it only took a glance at him approaching to warn them to expect to be pushed harder than of late!

Consequently he'd just started his warm-up routine when he was somewhat surprised by seeing two figures approaching. Telling Will to keep the others at it, he went across to meet Paul and his latest 'patient', Doug.

"Hello Doug. How are you settling in? Is our Paul here taking good care of you?"

"Yes thanks Mr Lockett. It's just good to have someone to talk to who understands me like Paul seems to."

"Oh, believe me, that's what he does best mate. I'd been in a hell of a state when he took me in hand, they had to practically lock me away until he got me sorted. Oh, and by the way, it's Steve, not Mr Lockett please."

Paul told Steve that Doug had heard of the exercise regime here, and it seemed he really wanted to join in.

"Are you sure you feel up to it mate? You really don't have to until you do feel up to it you know,"

Paul assured Steve that this had been Doug's idea. Having been kept away from the invasion yesterday, and had a good night in a small room next to Paul's, he was keen to get involved in the programme as soon as possible. Paul had explained to him that he shouldn't expect miracles; any recovery he made would only come after a fair length of time, but his answer to that was that, the sooner he started, the sooner it may happen.

Though Paul, as was his usual way, beat a retreat back to his quarters, Steve was pleased to take Doug along with the others (assigning Will to stay alongside of him to check on his ability to keep up). It seemed by the time they returned that there was little to worry about with Doug's physical condition. His problem was, as Steve's had been, purely psychological, and that would be purely down to our genius, Paul, to sort out.

Somewhat reluctantly, I'd forced myself out from the warmth of Steve's arms when he'd insisted on getting straight back to work, so I also set to and took the women's group. Though I'd been up and at them, full of energy and eagerness, when Steve was away, somehow this came harder today, but I have to admit that I did feel that bit better for doing so ... eventually!

On the whole it didn't seem so long before everyone was back, cleaned up, and eager for breakfast. I wondered at first just what the rush to get to the dining room was about, but then I realised that, once they'd actually got in there and sat down, it wasn't so much about the food for a change. No, this time the rush was purely so that they could be there in time to watch Tony Maningly's morning show! It struck me as amusing to think that, before all that had happened, it was unlikely that any of them had ever bothered to stick around long enough to do so, but then of course, neither had any of them seen Steve, let alone themselves on television before.

Though we sometimes would stay downstairs to eat with them, I had noticed that May was looking a little tired still from the previous day's events, so Steve and I decided to ask Josh to send our breakfast up to us. This was good as it gave us the opportunity to sit quietly around our table with her and eat breakfast while waiting to see just how we were all portrayed. Would Tony revert to his original stance of maintaining that our residents were the 'dregs of society', in spite of what he'd said yesterday? Had that just been because he perhaps felt intimidated by these people? After all, he could so easily put a totally different spin on the whole event if he chose to do so.

In my mind, and no doubt Steve's, I knew that if he did this it could have disastrous consequences for our work at the Grange. I was well aware that at this point our finances were only helped just a little by the odd small donation from one or two local firms who we'd supplied workers to when they were needed. Then of course, one of our main sources of income came from the functions we held here, but how many would choose to come here if they were given the wrong impression of us?

Though I tried hard to strike up some light-hearted conversation, it was clear we were all on edge, and for the same reason. The more I tried to chat away with any old rubbish, the less success I was having! Though I was almost dreading it, I must admit to being a little relieved when the programme did eventually begin. Of course, even then we still had to sit through all that political rubbish which is always at the beginning of these type of programmes. After this of course there were what seemed like everlasting adverts! I wanted to scream at the television like some demented fool, but somehow kept a casual smile up for the sake of May. When at last they announced that they would be showing 'Tony's adventures with Mr Steven Lockett, and giving his insight into the workings of Lansdown Grange', directly after the break, I couldn't help seeing an almost imperceptible shiver run through Steve, one which I could see that May did not noticed. I slipped my hand under the table and gave his a gentle squeeze to remind him that, whatever happened, he'd always have my support.

"Come on you two, let's get a front row seat. We might as well be comfortable on the sofa as sit here. No telling what the fool will have to say, but it can't make so much difference after all. It'll either have no affect at all, or it'll close us down for good. Can't do anything about it now."

He was doing his very best to sound as if he wasn't too bothered. In fact, and this was what was really tearing me apart, even after all that had been going on over these last weeks, I somehow knew he'd been trying for some months now to come to terms with the fact that he would be unable to keep the place going much longer. I knew that if he couldn't keep his work here going, perhaps even have to sell Lansdown, this could so easily break him. And then what? The effect of losing the work he'd achieved here over so long would most certainly destroy him! Since coming here and finding something he was good at, something to give him a true purpose, he'd also been able to completely rebuild what had become his own broken life, and one which I knew could never be truly forgotten. He had healed so many of his own wounds by helping others to heal theirs.

I tried my best to sound convincing, not to let him pick up on my concerns, but doubted he was fooled by me for a second, I never could lie to him and get away with it!

"Stop being so pessimistic Steve. He sounded pretty confident yesterday after all."

May agreed with me, and I must say that she did sound much more confident. In fact I couldn't help feeling her words held a certain tone of admonishment typical of a mother to a small boy!

"Yes son; Mel is quite right. You're not giving the man credit for appreciating all your hard work. Now come and sit next to me and stop acting like a child who can't get his own way!"

This did the trick. He stood there for a few seconds with a bewildered expression on his face, just looking down at us both sitting there each end of the sofa, before letting out a burst of genuine laughter and saying,

"Well, that's told me! As if one of you isn't bad enough, I've now got two of you having a go at me at the same time. Ok, shift up and let me in!"

We were both more than happy to do this. I couldn't help tipping a quick wink to May behind his back, by way of thanks for her support. She clearly understood the situation better than I'd given her credit for. It struck me that we do tend to think that, just because our parents are getting older, they no longer see or understand what is going on around them. I made a mental note to myself that I would never allow myself to do this again. After all, this is a lady who was responsible for giving birth to three sons and raising them alone for much of that time and, as I know so well, made such a brilliant job of this, and of her eldest in particular!

Somehow I felt that, not wanting to be seen to be in any way weak, or in need of female approval for anything, he appreciated knowing he had our backing come what may. He certainly need never have doubts on that score; we both loved the bones of the man, and would be behind him whatever was to come.

Downstairs too, all the hustle and bustle and general noise seemed to have stopped, and though I don't know if Steve noticed this, but I knew this meant that we were not the only ones desperate to hear what was to be said. After all, what happened next concerned all of them as much as us, though they probably had no idea that it could be the last straw for the place that meant so much to them all.

Chapter Thirty-Three

As the adverts finished and the camera focused again on Tony Maningly, across the whole of Lansdown a deathly silence descended. I'm sure you could have heard the proverbial pin drop! From the sofa he was seated on, Tony welcomed back viewers.

"As you may well know, a few weeks ago on this programme I was interviewing a chap by the name of Steven Lockett. He was here to talk about the work he carries on at his home, a place called Lansdown Grange. This turned out to be a large, Victorian mansion, which it seems he has completely renovated, sitting in a large expanse of grounds. In these he has increased its residential capacity by erecting a few small bungalows and a collection of pods.

As you may well remember, when he first came on my show to explain the work he did by taking in the homeless, those on drugs or drink, or with any other such problems, I own up to being rather dismissive of this idea … in fact thinking the man must be mad to waste his time on such … now, what did I call them? Ah yes, the dregs of society!

(I felt Steve tense up as he listened to this, but threw him a look which clearly said, BE PATIENT!)

Tony continued,

"Well, no doubt you'll remember Steve Lockett coming back to me with a challenge to spend a little time living rough with him, so that he could get me to understand some of the reasons for so many finding themselves in that position, and the problems they then have to face living with no help, and just what it is that Lansdown Grange and all those working there can do to help.

I must admit that at first I was rather reluctant to take up this challenge, but it seemed only fair to see both sides to the story, and so that was what I did. We will now show some of the footage from that time, mostly taken without my knowledge I must say, after which I will take a few questions from you, my viewers, on the number at the bottom of the screen. Oh, and by the way, you may not recognise me as Steve insisted I couldn't shave for some time before hand, and wore scruffy clothes to fit in!"

The footage they televised was pretty much what we'd seen yesterday, just overlaid with a quiet commentary by Tony where explanation was felt necessary. Give the man his due, he didn't pull any punches, actually making fun of himself on odd occasions! He took it right from when he'd found himself grabbed from his bed in the early hours, bundled blindfolded into the back of a van, and given no idea as to their destination.

He went to surprising lengths to tell of his attempt to scrounge something to eat the next morning, and just been given stale bread and mouldy cheese! He even allowed himself to lower his dignity sufficiently to describe that first night in the bus shelter!

He was honest about the chap they met first, who he'd thought must have been in on what was happening, and how, especially since returning to Lansdown, he had learnt that Steve had been truthful in assuring him that the poor chap was truly homeless. As Tony explained, this was when he learnt from that very man, just why he had nowhere to live. He went briefly through what had happened when this chap challenged him to go in the nearby job centre and ask for work, and that this was the point that he'd become aware of the 'no job, no money, therefore no home, and that no home address meant that no job syndrome!'

Thankfully very little was made of the way Steve had dealt with Tony's attackers, just saying how Steve had acted as his protector, and concentrating more on the need to find food and shelter. He also made a great deal of talking about what he'd learnt about the different attitudes of people toward those they saw as 'down and outs', and how this varied from pity to downright disgust!

Even so, there was no hiding the way Steve had handled the situation with poor Sarah. Though I know he still wasn't happy about her being flashed all over the television, meaning that her identity had been disguised even though she had actually told her story in her own words. It seemed she had personally given her permission to Tony to do so.

Though he had no footage of those living in the squat, which was no doubt a good thing for their sakes, he did talk briefly about this and the reasons that had brought them to be together there, and just how accepting they'd been for him, Steve and Sarah, to share this with them, even sharing what little food they had.

By this time I couldn't help glancing at Steve to get a measure of just what he was thinking so far. Knowing he was never very keen to do more than prove his point to Tony, not the whole television audience, I'd hardly dared look in his direction too often. I was reasonably content with his non-committal expression, so perhaps it was going pretty well!

The last part caught on film was from Bob's hidden camera, taken when Tony arrived at the final camp in the woods. It showed what certainly looked like a far more humble man than the one shown at the beginning of the time. It showed him handing over his dodgy vegetables and bread to Mia, and in return being more than happy to eat the meal she produced from them, something he'd never have considered before! In fact it was at this point that Tony added words by way of commentary telling the audience just how glad he was by this time to be given a share of their food, and in fact, just how good it had tasted after such a long day in the cold, and especially following the soaking he'd had that morning.

The film seemed to miss out any sign of Doug, quite probably due to a little editing by Bob, but moved on to show Steve arrive in the camp as they were all eating. Once again it stopped short of showing the part where Steve left his food to go to Doug's aid as it seems Steve had been adamant that this poor fellow had enough to contend with without being made a spectacle of in front of millions. Though Tony also understood the need to leave him in peace, in his mind he still had the picture of how genuinely understanding Steve had been and just how well he'd handled the situation, and this had made a big impact on the view he'd now formed of the man.

Of course, as you might guess, we then had to sit through more adverts! When the programme did resume it went on to the part I knew Steve was most concerned about, the part where the crew took their cameras around the whole estate, beginning with an interview with Josh and Mia, and a thorough look around, showing the immaculate kitchen and what remained of the amazing spread they'd laid out that afternoon.

From then it followed them on around to show the accommodation, beginning with the two long dormitories, both looking as clean and tidy as army barracks! A good number of the occupants were happy to stay in there to be interviewed, those not wishing to be taken out of harm's way before this began! Most of those occupying these quarters were the younger folk, and a good number were more than happy to explain just how they'd come to be here and give a good report of their time with us. This was really rewarding to hear, especially as we'd chosen to keep out of the way by this time, just leaving Will and our older residents to supervise from a safe distance, just to be sure they stuck to the policy of not opening any closed doors.

Those wandering off toward the gatehouse were met by Ellen, who was more than happy to invite a small group in. On the film we were quite surprised to watch as she openly told them the story of how, all those years ago, with Bob, Graham and young Jez, we had met up in the Grange where they'd been squatting for assorted reasons. She told of us coming in search of a place to shelter, but it was during that time Steve had come up with the idea of just what a great place it would be to set up somewhere for those in need of help. When one chap asked about Jez, she was quick to explain that with Steve's help to build up his confidence, he did get back to college to complete the course he had dropped out of before. All he needed was a push and encouragement from the right person, and that, as she made clear to them, was most definitely Steve!

As we sat there watching right through to the end of the filming I could feel Steve gradually relax into the sofa, but when I dared look round into his face I was a little shocked. I couldn't believe for a second that what I'd seen was just one small tear appearing!

"What's wrong Steve? Didn't you know how much they all think of you?

He tried hard to smile at me, but I knew this was forced. May had just gone off to the bathroom so hadn't heard my question. The look he threw me could almost be called pathetic!

"No, it's not that ... well, not entirely. The fools all count on me, and that just makes it worse. You must see that Mel?"

When I asked him what he meant by this I believe he came so close to crying openly.

"Well, if that's really how they feel, how the hell do I break the news to them? You know as well as I do that we can't afford to keep going much longer. And then what will they do, you tell me Mel ... just what will they do?"

Before I had chance to answer him, and before May came back, he got up and walked out. I heard him almost running down the stairs, heard the front door slam behind him, and knew there would be no point going after him! From our years together I knew that if he didn't want to be found, there'd be no point trying to. Just as May came back into the room Will came in at the door Steve had just left through. Both looked around the room, obviously with the same question on their lips, but it was Will who spoke first.

"Hey Mum, that was good wasn't it? They made a good job of it didn't they?"

He'd obviously come to say how everyone downstairs had enjoyed the viewing of Tony's adventures!

"Where's Dad gone? Did I just see him disappear out the front door? Will he be long; I think they're all waiting to see him."

May just stood in the doorway, obviously also waiting to hear the answer to Will's question. What should I say? I knew he wouldn't reappear until he was ready; after all it took two years before he surfaced once, and then that was probably due to my need for his help. This time I could feel his pain. After all the effort we, or should I say he, had put into developing the Grange into what it was now, if it did all crumble beneath his feet, I have no idea just what would happen.

I was about to put on a false smile and tell them he would be back soon ... but then, as I looked at May's face I could tell that she for one knew there was more to this than I was saying.

"Come in and shut the door Will. Both of you just come and sit down please."

"What is it Mel? There's something wrong, isn't there? Why has Steve gone out?"

There was that amazing motherly instinct again. I patted the sofa for Will to come and sit with us. As they sat there with me I told them what was worrying Steve. At first Will listened in bewilderment, before saying,

"I know things are not too good financially, but surely it's not that bad is it Mum? I mean, if we don't take in any more for a while, and still manage to find ways to help some get back out in the workforce, surely we can get it back on track can't we?"

I so wished I could agree with him, but I knew Steve had been trying to keep the true state of our finances from him for some time now. All I could do was be honest.

"So where has he gone? I'll go and find him and tell him we're all behind him, whatever happens. He can't just give up now can he? There must be a way somehow, after all, you know what he says ... where there's a will there's a way!"

I knew he'd be wasting his time, but what else could I say but yes, go and look for him, but I knew it was pointless!

Chapter Thirty-Four

We never did see the last part of Tony Maningly's programme that morning, assuming that after the last bunch of adverts he would move on to a different subject. I went down to show a brave face to the folk downstairs, not wishing them to catch on to what had happened. Meanwhile Chris (who had stayed on overnight rather than rush back to his place), and Will did a thorough scout around the whole estate. Though they left no stone unturned in their search I knew it would be pointless. Actually, I did think Chris might stand a better chance of finding him than Will, but it was not to be.

With much welcome support from Chris we managed to keep things going with as little disruption as possible for the rest of the morning. By midday though we decided to involve more people to help with our search. The groups doing the different activities, those hoping to become tradesmen eventually, were mostly finished for the day by then, so Will and Chris split them into two groups to do a circuit of the lake the other side of the woods. I wanted to go with them but Chris insisted I stay home in case he returned. Actually I believe he felt it best I shouldn't go for fear of what they might find, especially following a discussion with Paul about his state of mind. So I was banished to our room to keep May company while they took the two groups round, one each way, to meet the far end.

As I entered the room May was just putting the phone down. Though I knew this was a silly question, the first words from my mouth were,

"Was that Steve ringing?"

Of course it wasn't. I don't know why I'd said such a stupid thing when I knew he wouldn't! But then, as I told myself this, a thought rushed through my mind. I picked up my mobile, found his number, and pressed it, hoping he just might answer it ... but no; it did ring his, but the sound was coming from the sofa where he'd been sitting earlier! Damn, how many times have I stressed the need for him to keep it on him? But not him; oh no, he always did have the need to be, as he put it, a free spirit! The last thing he ever wanted was to be stuck to the end of a traceable gadget, that's what he always said. I had to stop myself letting out the stream of rude words (army style, learnt from you-know-who!), in front of poor May.

"No dear. Actually that call was from the television producer. After you went out I caught the tail end of the programme. Mr Manningly was trying to answer questions sent in by viewers, but after the first few he ran out of time. So he announced that they were going to invite Steve back on the show to join him in answering them. The call was from them to ask if he might be willing to do so at some point."

"Oh hell, you didn't tell them he's gone missing did you May? Or about his money worries?"

She looked decidedly sheepish at that last question!

"No, I just said he was out right now, and I'd get him to ring as soon as he had time."

I threw her a suspicious glance,

"And what about the money problems May? Did you say anything?"

"Well," she began warily, I did just say that I didn't know if he would want to bother under the circumstances. When he asked what I meant I, sort of accidentally you understand, commented that I think maybe he'd helped them earn money from what Steve did for Tony, when perhaps he could have used the time to try to save his own business. That's all I said ... I promise Mel."

What could I say? Bless her, she was Steve's mother alright! Even she could have that same edge as him when something or someone got under her skin, especially when this was in his defence!

By late afternoon the search party returned with no news of Steve. In spite of me attempting to keep the news of Steve's disappearance from as many as I could, this had proved impossible. While the two teams had searched round the lake, another unofficial group had got together and headed into the village to look and ask around amongst the locals, but it seemed that no one had seen him at all that day. This didn't surprise me at all. When Steve doesn't want to be found there's little chance of doing so.

Poor Will was quite distraught, but I persuaded him to go home to Lilly with a promise to call him if there was any news. I did a last walk around the place to see everyone was alright before going in for the night. Chris insisted on coming with me, he could tell just how I was feeling. I tried to look as reassuring as possible to those who popped their heads around their doors to say goodnight. Paul came out for a few words as we passed his place, and though he sounded confident when he told me not to worry, he'd be back when he was ready, somehow I couldn't bring myself to smile convincingly. Chris took me back up to our room where we found May had already turned in. The last two days had been quite an ordeal for her after all. We sat together with barely a word between us drinking a coffee until Chris said he too would take himself off to the bed he'd been given in the dormitory. I knew that at any other time, if Steve had been there, he would have joked about sharing with me to keep me warm. But that would have been to wind Steve up; I always knew I could trust him completely, but even so I must admit to a feeling of real comfort from the genuinely warm hug he gave me before going. Just as he opened the door he turned to say,

"Don't worry girl. You know old Steve … he'll be ok; and he'll be back before you know it."

Then he was gone, and I was left to spend a long sleepless night in that big cold bed, alone and scared as to what had happened to him, and where he was.

Early the next morning I was woken by the sound of our door opening. I gave a fleeting look at the clock. It was coming up to six o'clock, and I know the last time I'd looked it was about four fifteen, so I'd not been asleep long. Was that Steve? I called out to him, but not got the reply I was hoping for;

"No Mum, it's just me," said Will, "Didn't he come home at all then last night?"

He stuck his head around the door, almost as if he'd hoped to find Steve hiding under the bed clothes as he used to do when Will was small. I had to disappoint him this time. I told him to give me time to get dressed and I'd come and help with the exercise class. He did suggest we shouldn't bother with it today, but I was quick to assure him that Steve wouldn't be happy if we let things slip so to go and get them organised. By the time I'd taken May a drink to her room I was ready to go, though with little enthusiasm.

May had tried to sound as unperturbed as possible when she heard Steve had still made no appearance, and I could certainly sense an unrest amongst those waiting for me to join them outside. It was down to me to put on a brave face and convince them that everything was fine ... nothing to worry about! Lucky enough we still had Chris here to help lighten the mood with his usual way of clowning around to cheer things a bit.

By the time we finished our session, there was just time to shower and dress before breakfast time. Will had his with Lilly, but I asked Chris to come up and share it with May and myself. I think I was hoping he could have the same mood-lightening way with her too! I could tell that she was doing a valiant attempt at looking quite sure that all was well, but I knew this was just a front for my benefit. Poor Chris must have found it such hard going trying to keep any conversation up.

Not so long after this Will came back up to discuss, as he put it, strategy, to find Steve. We suggested that he should ask around to see how many want to join us in our hunt, and so he went off with Chris to ask around. He'd not been gone many minutes when the phone rang. I have no idea why I rushed to pick it up, but just as I did I hesitated. Suppose it was the police, or worse still, the hospital? What if he'd been in an accident and is injured ... or worse!

"Are you going to answer that Mel, or would you like me to dear?"

May's voice brought me to my senses. I snatched up the receiver just as I think it was about to stop ringing.

"Hello, am I speaking to Mrs Mel Lockett?

Not knowing who this was I said that I was,

The voice on the other end said,

"May I introduce myself? My name is Mick Ashley, Tony Maningly's producer. I believe we met the first time your husband appeared on the programme, and again when we came to your place at Lansdown Grange."

I felt myself already feeling the urge to say something rude and slam the phone down on him! Obviously I was more like May than I'd realised. My feeling was that I'd got too much to worry about trying to find Steve to worry about his damn show. But then I reminded myself that, to be fair to the man, he had no idea what was going on here.

"Right; what is it you want from Steve now?"

I must have sounded somewhat sharp, in spite of my attempt to be reasonably patient.

"Well, you see, I spoke to your mother-in-law yesterday and ... well, she gave me quite a stern telling off."

In spite of his words he did sound as if he'd taken her words in good part (thankfully!). Feeling a bit mixed between guilt and amusement, I waited for him to continue.

"Anyway, she said that your husband was out at the time. Is he available for a chat this morning at all?"

What should I say; should I lie and say he's gone for a walk, or that he's so exhausted from dragging Tony around that he's still in his bed? Or should I be truthful and tell him that the depression that has probably set off his old PTSD symptoms was caused by the business being so successful in its work that he's gradually running out of funds to carry it on, and that it's because of this that he's taken himself off and can't be found?

He waited patiently for my reply, but when I hesitated in deciding what to say, he changed tack and put another question entirely to me. It became clear that May's words hadn't fallen on deaf ears after all. I could tell immediately that he had obviously caught the sting in the tail of her rather sharp words. He repeated to me what she'd said about how he may have been better here trying to save his business rather than waste that time with Tony. He sounded genuinely sorry to think that we felt that they'd made money from this whilst our business was, as he now guessed, having a few financial problems!

A few ... how could I tell him the true depths of our problems? I felt that Steve would be fuming if he thought I'd made this public, as he saw it, telling the world what a failure he was. I knew that this was what he was thinking right now, and it was just that which had caused him to take himself off ... like a battle scarred lion, to lick his wounds in private!

Once again I'd been silent for so long that he took over the, rather one sided, conversation.

"Well, you see Mrs Lockett, or may I call you Mel?" He took my silence as agreement, "Mel, having watched the footage we shot of your business, plus that of Steve's time with Tony, we've been really impressed by the whole set-up you have there. We feel this shows a whole new concept of what can be done to help the homeless and less fortunate in society."

I nodded in agreement before remembering he couldn't actually see me, then quickly pulled myself together to say,

"Well, we like to think we've managed to make a bit of difference to quite a few."

I could almost hear a sigh of relief from him, knowing I might actually speak occasionally! "Well Mel, what we discussed with Tony, taking into account the overwhelming number of questions we've received from the viewers, that what we would love to do is to have yourself and Steve, and anyone else you care to bring along, back onto our show again, this time devoting the whole show to giving you chance to publicise your work and hold a Q&A with the viewers."

For a second or two I found myself speechless once more with the prospect of poor Steve even agreeing to this ordeal. Knowing how he'd hated the whole thing before, how the hell would he cope with this right now?

"You see," he went on, "from the feedback we've already received it seems there are people, both individuals and businesses, who are keen to invest money towards your running costs. So, what do you think Mel? Would you like to put the idea to Steve and get back to me later?"

What could I say? I chose to say nothing about Steve's disappearance, just that he was away at present, but that I would get back to him as soon as he returned and made a decision.

Chapter Thirty-Five

All we had to do now was find Steve. 'All' is a very small word, in this case at least, for a very big job! He'd been missing now for two days and two nights, and still there was no trace of him anywhere. The whole family was worried sick about him, everyone at the Grange had been frantically hunting around every corner of the place and beyond, like a pack of hounds on a hunt ... but there seemed no scent for them to follow! As for me, I found myself splitting my time between listening for that dreaded phone call, or trying to look as if I could cope for the sake of everyone else.

The one person I couldn't fool into believing my show of confidence was Chris. After all, he had known me longer than most, except perhaps for Paul. In fact, seeing the state of mind I was struggling so hard to control, it was Chris who suggested we should pop in to have a word with Paul that morning. I didn't see what good this would do, but I did know that Paul had been a big support to Steve through the worst of his recovery originally.

When we got to his bungalow he was sitting chatting to Doug but they were happy for us to join them. Though Doug had not been with us more than a few days, it seemed he'd already begun to find great comfort in Paul's company and counselling. Of course, like the rest around here, they were well aware of Steve's disappearance. Doug was genuinely sympathetic.

"I'm so sorry Mrs Lockett, Mel. It can't have helped him being faced with me in the state I'm in. Paul's been explaining just what a battle your poor husband had to go through to make the recovery he has. And before you say ... I do know it'll probably never go away completely."

"No, you're right Doug, there's always a bit lurking in the background; and no, you don't have a bearing on what's happened. I wish it was that simple."

Paul handed us both a coffee and asked if there was any news ... of course there wasn't. He tried a few suggestions, but they were all places someone had looked. It seemed that when they had been round, looking in the sort of nooks and crannies that Doug reckoned were the sort of places he would have hidden, even these had proved fruitless. Just as we were leaving Paul did offer a few words of advice which, at first thought, seemed a bit too obvious to help. Anyway, I thought I must already have asked this. He said I should ask May, sitting quietly with her so as not to wind her up or upset her, if Steve had ever mentioned anywhere in particular he liked to go to think when he had a problem. I did promise to try, but wasn't at all optimistic about getting any results from it.

By the time we got back to our quarters for breakfast, one I really couldn't stomach had it not been for my attempt to put on a brave face for May. Though I knew Chris felt as concerned as I was, he hid it well behind a plate of bacon and egg courtesy of Josh, and the cheery face he managed to put on for our sake! All I could manage was one slice of toast and a glass of orange juice.

Having had his breakfast with Lilly, Will came up to ask what the plan for the day was, and could I think of anywhere he could take a gang to search? All I could suggest was that perhaps they could cover the woods on the far side of the village, though somehow I knew this would prove fruitless. But then, it would make him feel better just to think he was doing something useful.

I could see he was beginning to panic, and perhaps even accept he would never see his father alive again. Chris also sensed this, but put on a very positive tone telling him,

"Don't look so worried son; wherever he is he'll be fine. He'll come creeping back to get the rough edge of your mother's tongue when he's ready! Just remember that the training we had all those years ago taught us how to stay hidden for days. He'll be ok lad."

I believe he did wonder whether to go with Will, but decided that I might need support, and so, while May and I sat quietly chatting, he took the remains of the breakfast things down to the kitchen.

I waited for him to come back before asking, as casually as I could, if she'd ever heard Steve talk of a place he'd go to think? She said that she really couldn't say that she had, and then added,

"Well, certainly not since coming to live here dear."

And then she smiled a wry smile, almost to herself, and said,

"Not like when he was a boy. Then if he had anything worrying him it was always his father, Peter, he would go to."

That's it! The one place we hadn't looked ... but then, I asked her,

"But he didn't know where his father was buried did he May? He was away when we went up to the cemetery last week, wasn't he?"

"I'm not sure dear, but it's possible that he may have remembered. You see, when Peter passed away he had always requested that he should be brought back to the family plot. Though Steve was only fifteen at the time, when a friend of mine was kind enough to offer to bring me up to here to have his ashes interred as he'd wished, young Steve insisted on coming along to support me. We've never been back here since, and I've never said anything to remind him it was here, but perhaps it's possible he found it since you came here?"

That was all we needed to hear; with barely another word, just a quick kiss on her cheek, poor May watched in amazement as we leapt to our feet, threw on our coats and rushed out the door! The little church on the hill was about eight miles away, so I'd grabbed the car keys on the way out, just hoping that our hunch might pay out. I went to get in the driver's door, but Chris took the keys and insisted on driving as he could see I was really in no fit state to do so. He was probably right, I could feel myself shaking in anticipation ... or was it dread as to what we might find? After all, Steve had been gone nearly three days now, and for two particularly cold nights. Though I knew from experience that he was easily capable of coping when he was in a good frame of mind that was the last thing he in was right now!

The church on the hill was rarely attended during the week which would have meant that it would be highly unlikely that anyone visited except for Sundays or special days. But this was Thursday. Even the vicar lived a way off and only went there when he had a service to conduct, and so we knew that, if Steve was there, there was a good chance he wouldn't be seen by anyone for a few more days.

"Stop worrying until you know what to worry about girl," Chris threw a sideways glance as we sped off up the hill. "Anyway, surely if he's there he'd have the sense to get inside the church?"

"Well, I can see you're not a church goer Chris," I managed to say with half a grin, "Or you'd know they lock them up these days when there's nothing going on!"

He did his best to keep my hopes up, if nothing else, by pulling a face at me!

I've never known such a short drive appear to take so long, but eventually we did arrive. As we went in through the gate I looked around, desperately trying to remember where, amongst so many stones, was Steve's father buried. It took Chris' firm hand on my shoulder to calm me sufficiently to think methodically.

Then, as we headed in the direction my muddled head was telling me, I saw something that sent a cold shiver down my spine!

"Oh God no! Over here Chris, he's over here and I think he's …"

I couldn't bring myself to say the word I was thinking. All I could see as I rushed towards him was a cold, lifeless body, slumped against the gravestone. I reached him seconds before Chris, to find him, if not dead, certainly appearing unconscious, and with two empty whisky bottles on the ground beside him!

By this time Chris was kneeling by my side, checking Steve over thoroughly. Putting a calming hand on my arm he assured me that Steve wasn't dead, he still had a pulse (a very weak one mind you), and was probably kept warm by the whisky he'd drunk!

"Quick girl, go back to the car and fetch the rug from the back seat. We need to get him warmed up a bit smartish."

As I dashed off I heard him talking to Steve,

"Come on man, pull yourself together. We've been through worse than this, besides, you can't leave Mel now or ... well I'll have to take her over, and you wouldn't like that now would you mate?"

By the time I got back with the rug Chris had Steve propped against him rather than the stone, though still showing little sign of response. He wrapped the rug around Steve and told me to keep rubbing and talking to Steve while he rang for an ambulance.

I didn't need asking twice, only too glad to put my arms around the person who means the most to me in the world. Though I was talking to him, inside I was praying that he would come through this, and that it wouldn't set him back to that truly awful state he'd fought so hard to get through!

Though I could feel Steve's heartbeat, it felt pretty weak, and he'd still not made any real response. When Chris came back over to me he didn't have any good news. It seemed that the nearest ambulance was half an hour away, and would then take a fair while to get him to the hospital.

"I'm not prepared to risk waiting that long Mel. We'll have to take him there ourselves in the car. Can you help me get him up on his feet?"

I would do anything right then if it was what needed doing to save him, but I felt somewhat redundant when, having helped haul him up off the ground, Chris bent down and pulled Steve onto his back to carry him to the car! At any other time I probably would have made some silly remark about him looking like a big bear, carrying its prey back to its lair, but this wasn't appropriate right then.

I opened the back door of the car for him to put Steve in, going round the opposite side to help pull him. I decided to sit in the back to nurse his head in my lap, and to help keep him warm, whilst directing Chris the best I could remember to Coventry hospital. Just as we hit the outskirts though, travelling at the breakneck speed Chris had been driving, we found blue lights coming by us and found ourselves pulled over by a police car!

Chris leapt out to speak to them, telling me to sit tight. One chap came over and peeped in at me sitting with poor Steve in the back seat, and this seemed to do the trick. The next thing I knew, Chris jumped back in, called over his shoulder,

"Hang on tight girl, we've got ourselves a police escort."

He was certainly right there! If I'd not been so worried about Steve I would have been terrified at the even faster speed we were travelling at, right through the busy traffic, nonstop until we pulled up outside A&E, where a trolley, doctors and nurses were all standing by. Before I could barely extract myself from the car they had whisked poor Steve away, leaving me with Chris to put an arm round my shaking body and follow them in. I wanted to stay with him, but they closed the door and all I could do was stand outside and watch what I could see of the activity through the blinds half pulled at the window.

"He's going to be fine Mel, just give them time to get his body temperature up and re-hydrate him. Look, you sit here while I get you a cuppa and then I'll give young Will a call. He can break the good news to May. She must be wondering what's going on by now, especially after the way we rushed out in such a hurry eh?"

"Ok Chris, and thanks, I don't know what I'd have done without you today."

He gave me a quick hug and just said, "Any time girl," and walked off to find a drink machine!

Chapter Thirty-Six

By the time I was half way down the hot tea Chris had brought me the doctor who had been in with Steve came out.

"Mrs Lockett, I'm pleased to say that your husband is doing well. He was just suffering from a touch of hypothermia and a little too much whisky ... though I suspect that helped protect him from the worst of the hypothermia! The nurse will be out shortly to fetch you."

It seemed like an age before the door opened again and a kind looking nurse appeared. She looked around to find me, but I was there by her side before she needed to look further.

"Is he going to be ok? Can I come in now please?"

The poor girl must have felt she was being attacked by some mad woman, but even so, she just smiled sweetly and said that I could.

"Just try not to tire him though, he's still a bit 'out of it', and will be rather weak for a while due to too much alcohol on an empty stomach."

Any other time I may have seen the funny side of this, but right then I was feeling a mixture of relief tinged with concern, and downright fury at him for the worry he'd caused everyone who cared for him! After all, even if he hadn't given it consideration, I knew that the whole population of Lansdown Grange would be heaving a huge sigh of relief by now. I'm sure he had never truly understood the depth of feeling they all had for this man for what he'd done for every one of them.

I went in through the door, intent on tearing him off a strip for his stupid behaviour, but as soon as I saw him lying there, cleaned up, tucked up warmly, and with a drip feeding fluids into him, I knew there was no way I could do this. All I could do was go to him and take hold of the lifeless arm protruding from the covers.

"Mel ... is that you my love?"

And then those big brown eyes opened and looked in my direction. All thoughts of reprimanding him in any way just melted into that pool of brown!

"Yes Steve, it's me. You're ok now; just rest and let them help you my love."

After all, there'd be plenty of time to tell him off later, when he was up to it. He took hold of my hand as I went to pull the covers a little higher, pulled me toward him, and whispered "sorry" in my ear, then found the strength from somewhere to give me a quick kiss. Of course it was just at that moment that Chris popped his head round the door.

"Ok, I see there's life in the old dog yet! Put her down man or they'll be throwing you out."

This remark had the effect of lightening the mood, and was lightened even more by his words which though humorous, also carried what I sensed was his way of reprimanding Steve,

"One more bout of that sort of behaviour though mate and I promise I will take the poor girl off you for good. Do you hear what I'm saying?"

Steve threw him the briefest of looks which would have offered a threat to any lesser man, before giving way to a broad grin and saying,

"Yes Sir! I hear what you're saying mate. And thanks by the way. They tell me I've got you to thank for helping Mel and for getting me here."

Chris grinned broadly and told him about the police escort,

"Bloody good fun driving at that speed though the streets behind a blue light. Might even apply to join the force as a driver."

"They wouldn't have you. You're too old and too reckless." Steve threw back.

Looking round at me Chris said,

"I'll go outside and wait for Will. He insisted on coming. Anyway, you no doubt have plenty to ... um... talk about!"

Now and again the nurse popped in to check on the drip and Steve's general condition. The rest of the time, especially knowing Will (and most probably May), would want to spend a little time with him, I just sat quietly, holding his hand. After all, there'd be plenty of time for talk later, when he'd recovered. I did wonder about breaking the news to him about the television programme that had been suggested, but decided this could work one of two ways; either it would give him fresh hope to resolve the financial problems, or it just could tip him over the edge completely! No, that could wait.

When the rest of the family arrived it seemed that Chris had filled them in on the situation, and had explained that Steve wasn't to be stressed, so to keep the conversation as light as possible. Once I could be sure that they, Will in particular, had been informed of this, I left the room as we'd been told no more than two people at a time should be there.

Once again, there was Chris, sitting in the waiting area with more hot drinks, his solution to most situations, so it seemed.

As we sat there in silence, sipping away at our drinks, I took what was possibly my first 'real' look at this man. Steve's best friend, always there to help in any situation, and equally strong minded and capable as Steve. It wasn't hard to see that they'd both spent much of their adulthood in all the hard, and often dangerous, conflicts whilst serving in the paras. This had obviously helped to form an unbreakable bond, rarely found in any ordinary men.

Being married to Steve had meant that Chris had been happy to include me in that tight circle of friendship, and of this I will always be so grateful. I knew once again that, if I ever needed the sort of strength and support that Steve gave me, there would always be this man sitting next to me to fall back on. I'd known for many years now that his wife had divorced him some years ago now, and had taken their two children to New Zealand with her new husband, but he'd grown to accept the odd video chat with them now knowing that, as he saw it, they were having a better life there. I must admit that I'd always thought he seemed happier as a bachelor, but perhaps I was wrong.

"Chris," he looked up from his cup and waited for me to go on, "Did you mean what you said to Steve just now … about how," I hesitated, "about how you would take me off him … only you've said things like that before."

What the hell was I doing? Whatever made me even ask when I knew there's no way on earth either Chris or anyone else could persuade me to leave Steve, no matter what happened!

As fond as I was, and as grateful to him for him being there when I needed him, at that very moment I wished I'd not said that. If I couldn't have my Steve, of course I didn't want anyone else! I believe it was just a spur of the moment reaction to his ability to give me the same protected feeling I'd always found with Steve. After all, I'd loved my fiancée, Jake, before meeting Steve, and before he was murdered, but now I think back to those long forgotten days it was clear that there was no comparison between them. Poor Jake might have been a fantastic business man, and he certainly loved me ... in his own way; nothing like the full on, undivided love I'd always felt from Steve.

Yet here I was doing this; doing what? Making a pass at his best friend! Oh my God, that's not what I'd meant to do at all.

"Oh dear. I... well I ... I didn't mean to ..."

I dared to look up at him, just as he looked down at me with a serious expression on his face! Oh no, he thought I'd meant it. I wouldn't be surprised if he didn't grab me and plant a kiss on me there and then. He held that serious expression for just long enough to convince me that he was about to do just that before bursting into raucous laughter and saying,

"Well, that's the best offer I've had for ages girl, but I'll have to say no for three reasons. I know you don't really mean it, and anyway, I'm not the marrying kind, been there, done that."

When I asked what the third reason was, he said,

"Ain't that pretty obvious? He'd kill me sooner than let me take you off him!"

None the less, I still gave him a 'sisterly' peck on the cheek and thanked him once more for being there when Steve needed him most.

"Aw, go on; he'd do the same for me," and as an afterthought, added, "but then, I don't deliberately get in such positions in the first place. Even so I promise you, he's got the courage, and the strength when he's called on to use it, or I wouldn't be here now!"

By this time he had walked me back to the car, still parked in a space marked 'Doctors Only', I'd processed his last words. Once we were well out of town on the quieter roads I asked him what he'd meant by his last remark. The story he told me sent shivers down my back!

It seemed that when they were fighting the Taliban on their first tour of duty, the two of them had been amongst the front line, but as they retreated thinking the enemy had gone, Chris had been bringing up the rear. It was then that he'd been ambushed by stray enemy who, for whatever reason, decided to shoot him in both legs to prevent him getting back to the British lines. Steve saw what had happened and had opened fire alone to drive them off. With Chris unable to stand, let alone walk, Steve had pulled him up onto his back and carried him the five hundred yards or so back to safety! By the time Chris was back on his feet and well enough to return to duty, Steve and the rest of the group were already on their second tour.

Chapter Thirty-Seven

All at the Grange were much relieved that night when we arrived home. Much against my better judgement we had to leave Steve there at the hospital overnight, but, due to a remarkably fast recovery, they said we could collect him around midday the next day to allow the doctors to do their rounds first.

As Chris had no intention of leaving us until he knew Steve was back on his feet, and Will and the senior members of our staff were managing, I found myself able to stay in with May that morning. Poor May had been through quite an ordeal, never having seen her beloved son in the state he was in. It was true that Paul had spoken to her, both when Steve had been at the centre, and since he'd come here, to explain to her just what effects of PTSD were, but this was the first time she'd experienced the way it could cause him to be fine one minute, yet do a complete flip the next, losing all grip on self-control.

"Oh dear, my poor dear. So that was why he got so upset after the television show. Surely there must be some way we can help him find a way to raise a little more money?"

I heaved a sigh. As I explained to her, the producer chap had hinted that there were a few people showing an interest in making a contribution, but then would this be enough, and would Steve accept what he looked on as charity?

"Nonsense!" said May, "If he wants to keep up his good work here he should be grateful for any offer of help, silly boy!"

This remark brought a smile to my face, probably the first for quite a few hours now. Typical mothers remark!

We'd barely finished breakfast when the phone rang. I rushed straight to it almost in a panic in case something had happened to Steve! Of course it wasn't; what a relief? The familiar voice on the other end introduced himself,

"Hello Mel. It's Tony Maningly here. How are you today?"

So much for the niceties I thought. For a second my instinct was to say b.....o, well, you know; but I resisted the urge and just said good morning instead.

"I hope you don't mind me intruding on you just now, but I was a little worried about Steve. My producer tells me that he'd spoken to you a few days ago, and you'd promised to get Steve to ring back. I was rather concerned. Is he ill; or have we upset him with our programme last week?"

Now I really was lost for words. Should I lie, or maybe it would be best to just come straight out with it and tell the truth. Before I could decide just what to say, Tony's voice came back again,

"Forgive me if I'm appearing impertinent Mel, but having got to know your husband, I really would like the opportunity to apologise for my initial attitude to what he does there. And although I never said anything to him, I was lucky enough to gain a deeper insight into Steve himself, and his background."

This was beginning to sound worrying. What did he mean by that? I waited for him to go on.

"You see, I had the privilege to see the expert and caring way he dealt with that poor chap with PTSD. It wasn't until then that I learnt from Mia that Steve has had the same thing. Is that correct?"

"Well, not so much 'had', more a case of 'has'. You see, from what our counsellor tells me, it's unlikely this will ever go completely. More a case of learning to live with it and control it."

I was going to go no further, but then I thought it was only fair to give some explanation of what was going on here, so I took my life in my hands, as it were, and jumped in feet first!

"Actually Tony, and bear in mind he'll be fuming if he knows I've told you this, but that is exactly why he's not got back to you."

Before I could stop myself I'd told him the whole story of how, though at first Steve had been pleased how well Lansdown and our work here had come over on television, that it was this that had brought to the fore in Steve's mind that this was going to make it all the harder to tell everyone here that we were probably going to have to let them down by closing the place due to lack of funds.

He listened in almost stunned silence, obviously finding this hard to take in. I then found myself thinking, in for a penny in for a pound, and went on to explain how this worry had pushed him back into possibly the worst attack of PTSD he'd suffered for years! As I explained, this place and his work had given him purpose and something to focus on since we began. When he asked in what way this was manifesting itself, what could I do but talk him through the events since the fatal day when Steve had walked out on us.

"Oh my, I have to admit I had no idea about this. Is he ok now Mel?"

I explained that we were fetching him home later in the day, but as for the PTSD, I could only hope we could find a way to get him through it. He hesitated before saying what he was clearly wondering if he should say.

"Well Mel, now I believe I may be in a position to offer a solution to that if you think it's the finances that are his biggest worry."

"That's kind of you Tony; your producer did say he knew a few people wanted to send us a little. But I'm afraid it's far more than a little one off hand-out we need. Poor Steve has used every drop of money he was left with the house, plus a chunk from a charitable start-up payment, and on top of that we put in most of our own money each month. A certain amount comes in from running weddings, conferences etc., but these can't be counted on as regular payments. No ... I think Steve is right, we're sinking fast!"

"Whoa there Mel ... you're getting ahead of me. I'm not talking a few people with a small amount. In fact there is one in particular who is the managing director of a multi-national company, plus at least another two, both big business men. There are also two or three who say they'd be interested in taking on a couple of apprentices if you have any interested youngsters. Well ... what do you think Mel? Does that sound like a solution to some of your problems do you think?"

Wow! That certainly sounded pretty good to me. But then it's not me that needed convincing. I knew that it would all depend on how Steve looked on the idea. I knew he'd never accept charity as such, but then that was not what was on offer here. I explained this to Tony, but it seemed he'd already worked that one out! As he said, it hadn't been until spending time on the streets with Steve that he'd understood how impossible it was to find employment without an address to register, but it was our ability to furnish them with this, be it rather grand, one which he now realised quite obviously made it possible for so many to get back into the world of work.

"Look Mel, I know you're more concerned with getting Steve home and back on his feet, so I'll leave this in your hands to sound him out on the idea when you see fit. Meanwhile we'll just mention on the programme that, due to unforeseen circumstances, the proposed return of Steve on the show has had to be postponed. That way it will give you breathing space to try to talk him round."

At last I could see a light at the end of the very dark tunnel! All I had to do now was to find a way to talk Steve round … that was all!

But that could wait. Right at that moment all I could think of was getting to the hospital to bring my man home where he belongs. Will would have taken me but I suggested he should stay to run things until his father was up to taking the reins again, and so it was down to Chris to act as my driver! I did say I could manage on my own, but I think he felt my mind just might not be entirely on the road that morning. He was quite possibly right, I doubt I'd have been particularly safe.

"After all, the plan is to bring someone home from the hospital, not put two back in it!"

I must admit to being quite pleased to be driven as my mind wasn't exactly on the road. All the way there my head was spinning with thoughts of having my man home again, but also with just how I was going to persuade him to consider the offers of help Tony had told me about earlier.

Chapter Thirty-Eight

I decided to take the coward's way out and say nothing that day about Tony's call. I was so pleased to find Steve up on his feet and walking about as if nothing had happened when we arrived. It seemed that all the staff had, in spite of his drunken orgy, been falling over one another in their rush to see to his every need! When we went through his door he had two nurses there with him, chatting away as if he was the only patient in the ward! In fact the younger of the two was just standing there looking on with what could only be described as a look of adoration! The more mature of the two was helping him on with his jacket which had obviously been well dried from his exploits.

I was never so glad to feel his arms thrown around me just then, even if I was somewhat embarrassed when he chose to plant on me a kiss so full of meaning in front of both nurses and Chris. I couldn't help glancing over his shoulder as he released me, in time to catch a look of sheer longing on the face of the younger nurse! Bless her.

We stopped on our way out for the doctor to give Steve some tablets to ward off any side effects (though I knew they'd end up in the bin), and headed for the car. I think Steve would have liked to drive, but Chris put his foot down firmly and suggested we'd perhaps be better with him behind the wheel this time! Secretly I think he was hoping he could get another blue light drive like the previous day, but that wasn't going to happen. Anyway, I was glad to take his suggestion and sit in the back with Steve. The feel of his arm round me made me wish that Lansdown was quite a lot further away.

When we did get there though, we had quite a surprise ... Bob saw us coming and opened the gate for Chris to drive straight in, and as we travelled up toward the house, the driveway and space outside the Grange itself was full of all our amazing residents, all out to cheer and wave, keen to welcome Steve home and show him their support! And as we pulled up by the door, Will, Lilly and May were there in the doorway too.

Dear May threw caution to the wind the minute Steve stepped out of the car and came across to throw her arms around him. It was clear to see the tears running down her cheeks, tears that were joined by those of her son. I discreetly handed him a tissue from the box in the car, and watched on as this big, strong, independent man, tenderly wiped the tears away from the cheeks of his mother in the same way that she no doubt did for him when he was a small child.

"Sorry Mum, I didn't mean to upset you like this. I know what you're thinking ... I'm old enough to know better."

May looked up at him, gave him a slap on his arm, and told him,

"Yes son, you really are. Do you have any idea of the upset you've caused me? Not just me either, just look at all these folk so pleased to see you."

Steve looked, rather sheepishly, around at the crowd gathered there to welcome him home.

"Yes, sorry Mum, and sorry to all of you for the way I've behaved. I admit we have a few problems to sort out, and I just let them get on top of me, but I know there's got to be a solution ... and as my son told me, I won't find it at the bottom of a bottle!"

Will and Lilly took May back upstairs while Chris and I stayed with Steve while he accepted all the handshakes and cheery words from the crowd gathered outside before joining them there. By that time Lilly had made hot drinks for us all, which gave me the opportunity to produce the bottle of tablets from Steve's jacket and hand him one.

"No Mel, I don't want them. I'm not keen on taking things I don't need."

Before I had chance to answer him, May looked up from her drink, shook her finger at him, and told him,

"Just for once young man, do as you're told! I think you've caused poor Mel enough worry for a while, don't you?"

He promptly took the tablet and swallowed it, opening his mouth to prove to her it had gone! Yes ... my Steve was back. Still the problems need tackling, but he still has that wicked sense of humour somewhere buried inside him.

Chris popped up to sit with Steve for a time later. When Steve asked if he needed to get back to his leisure centre business, Chris said that he had backed off quite a lot now as he had appointed a pretty capable manager to supervise and keep the staff up to scratch. He asked if it would be helpful for him to stay on for a while to help Will keep things running so Steve could have a bit of a break. Secretly I couldn't help thinking that he was enjoying our company, and I felt Steve was more than happy to have him around. I'm sure that this was due to the hardships they'd endure together from their army days forming such a unique bond. As there was no problem finding him somewhere to stay we were happy to say yes.

And so, with great difficulty, I prised Steve away from his determination to almost run everything single handed, and let Chris and Will take much of the burden for a while!

The next morning Ellen took Lilly and May off into Coventry to buy more baby things. After all, you can never have enough! Knowing that Chris had gone to help Will gave me the opportunity I'd been waiting for ... or should I say, dreading? Having found a (particularly fantastic) way to keep Steve in bed somewhat longer than usual, I knew I'd finally got him in a relaxed and mellow frame of mind! After all, you can't stay married to the likes of Steve for so long without learning just how to achieve this. In fact, now we were completely alone for once, we'd even taken advantage of our, particularly roomy shower and ... well, economised on water!

It was now or never, I promised Tony I'd try, so here goes nothing!

Chapter Thirty-Nine

I handed him a much needed drink before starting my quest.

"Steve, I ..." he looked me straight in the eye with those big brown ones of his, "Well, you see, while you were away,"

I hesitated, and then remembered the old adage, 'he who hesitates is lost', so took a deep breath and, trying not to look directly into those eyes, continued to explain some of what Tony had said. Somehow I knew before I'd opened my mouth, just what would happen. He would attack in a way reminiscent of a lion whose tail had been pulled!

"Now look; you know bloody well; there's no way on this earth I'm accepting charity. You had no right to tell that man I would!"

"No, you just wait will you? I haven't explained it properly yet, and besides, he wasn't talking of charity. What he said was ..."

"I don't care what that fool said. All he wants is to make money for himself and that bloody programme. How's that not charity may I ask? Anyway, the answer is NO!"

At this point he stood up and was crossing the room to storm out of the door, but I had got this far and had absolutely no intention of letting him walk out again. I beat him across the room and stood firmly between him and the door.

"Oh no you don't, don't even think of taking off again! Sit down and listen properly. You're being too judgmental. At the very least you could have the courtesy to listen to the whole thing before you throw another tantrum!"

Well, sometimes you have to fight fire with fire. There was no way, now I'd got him sitting there like a scolded kid, that I was about to let him run away from what I wanted to say. I believe I could see a scowl on his face, but I knew that I'd got just this one chance of getting through to him. If he walked out of the room now I'd lost the battle ... which ultimately could mean us losing everything we'd worked for all these years! No, I was not prepared to do that when there just may be a solution on offer.

Now I'd got his attention I took a breath and carried on, making him hear what Tony had told me about the chap from the multi-national company plus a handful of other similar ones, all keen to invest, and also be pleased to take on the odd apprentices as the opportunity arose. They had even gone so far as to say that some of these places came with accommodation for the right youngsters. After all, it seems that the managing director of this large company had started his early life working odd shifts on a market until he'd got a break offered by someone.

Besides all of this I explained, and this with great trepidation, Tony felt he would still be keen to have Steve and anyone we cared to take along, to go back on his programme once more. As he said, partly to apologise in public for his initial attitude to Steve and his work, but also to make public that we may be setting up a trust, backed by a handful of large businesses, to help fund the work carried on at the Grange.

By the time I'd come to the end of my speech I dared look at his face for the first time. Until then I had been standing over him, attacking him with words, but not daring to look down! When I finally stopped I braved his wrath by looking down at him, waiting for him to do or say something. I wouldn't have been surprised if he'd got up, pushed me out of the way, and gone; or maybe just bellowed at me! Hesitantly, I waited for some reaction, but when I dared look down at him I could see that he was thinking about my lecture! What now?

"I don't know Mel. All I can do is give it some thought. If I let people invest it won't be long before they take over; and then what'll happen? After all, this is our home, and when we're gone it'll be Will, Lilly and their baby who will inherit it. I can't risk just giving it away to just any old millionaire who takes a fancy to it."

Though I could see where he was coming from, I still felt there must be a way to ensure this never happened. If we could just get him to agree to discuss it with Tony, and perhaps he could call on his own solicitor brother, Tom, to investigate the advantages or risks before agreeing to anything definite. Having at last got him to sit there and listen to what I had to say I could see that he just may at the very least agree to think about it and not just miss out on what could be a life-saver as far as Lansdown was concerned. I knew exactly how he felt about the place, but more importantly, the work we did there but, as I put to him, if he insisted on being too proud to consider help when it was offered, we could quite well have to close it down; and then what? The Grange had been a deserted and dilapidated wreck that day we first found it; did he really want to see it going back to that state again?

"Ok, ok; I hear what you're saying Mel. I'll ring Tony later and have a chat, but I warn you, there's absolutely no way I'm letting anyone take over how we run the place, and certainly not take ownership of it! You had a good point about talking to Tom, perhaps he can look into how we can accept help without losing control. Anyway, it's about time we had a catch-up. I'll ring him too this morning and see if he can spare time to come over and chat before we commit to anything."

"Good idea," I said, as if it had been his, "Leave it to me. You can go out and see what's going on outside now … that is unless all that thinking has made you tired enough to go back to bed for a while!"

"Um; come to think of it I am still …"

"No, I was kidding! Go on, before they come looking for you."

"But we could lock the bedroom door and pretend we're not there."

It was all I could do to say no to his last remark!

But no, I told myself. I must stay strong and kick him out to show his face outside or, with the exception of Chris (who will no doubt have guessed), they will all be wondering what's keeping him up here on what seems a bright morning. As I told him, he would need to ring Tony after eleven, when the programme was finished and he was free to talk.

Meanwhile I decided to ring Tom to explain our situation and ask his advice on the suggestion Tony had made about allowing these business men to invest money in our work. As I told him, our Will was already getting to grips with the business side of the work here, and would be capable of keeping a watchful eye on the Lansdown accounts, but I knew we needed help on the legal side of things. He asked why we were considering the idea of allowing financial backers, so I knew I had to fill him in about the full situation and the effects it was having on poor Steve. Straight away I could tell in his voice just how much this worried him. I couldn't help thinking what a sensitive and concerned brother he was to Steve.

"Well Mel, I can see your situation is a great worry to you both. But I reckon, if you leave it to me to look in to, I can probably work out the best and safest way to do what you need and accept help, without the risk of doing what Steve would hate, and losing ownership or control of Lansdown Grange. After the work you've put into it over the years it would be wrong to do that."

I heaved a sigh of relief on hearing his words of assurance.

"Thanks Tom. Somehow I knew we could come to you for advice. If anyone can help us it would be you. I think you're the one person Steve would trust with this anyway; you know what a stubborn beast he can be when he puts his mind to something?"

"Do you really think so Mel? What our Steve … the same one who wouldn't come home for two years!"

Chapter Forty

Later that morning Steve appeared back in our room. Even after me assuring him that I'd spoken to Tom, and that he had felt pretty certain he would be able to find a way to let us accept financial help without risk to Lansdown, I still had to practically dial the number of Tony's studio and put it into Steve's hand with a stern, almost threatening, look on my face!

I stood over him just to make sure he couldn't chicken out or say there was no answer, until I heard him actually ask to speak to Tony. I was afraid that if I turned my back he'd find some silly excuse, and I had no intention of allowing him to let go of what was clearly a lifeline for us all. In fact, last night when we were alone, I had even put to him the worry this was to May. As I reminded him, she'd given up her home to Jamie and Sally, and so would be homeless like the rest of us if he let his pride prevent him from listening to what was suggested.

Whilst he stood with the phone in his hand, as if to reinforce that sentiment, as if she'd heard me saying this, May came into the room. She came armed with her knitting, more baby clothes I believe, and placed herself firmly on the sofa in sight of her son. I do believe that this was her way of intimidating him into doing as he was told!

Either way, I was glad to see that he'd taken us seriously and did actually wait to be connected to the man in question, and then I went across the room to sit alongside May, hopefully forming an impenetrable barrier between Steve and the door to prevent escape! Somehow I knew now that he realised that, just for once in his life, he needed help. After all the help he'd given to so many over the years, now it was time to accept some himself.

Without trying not to look too threatening, I glanced across from time to time, unable to hear Tony's part of the conversation, but smiling a supportive smile at my man, knowing just how difficult it was for him to even consider accepting help. To him it was admitting to failure, but we all knew that this certainly wasn't the case, in fact any lesser man would have given up years ago. It was only Steve's strength, determination, and downright hard work that had kept it going this long. I knew now that our future was down to this conversation and how Steve accepted the idea of, at the very least, listening and considering what was offered.

After the frustrating position of sitting there listening to one end of a conversation, I was relieved to see Steve sound as if he would agree to go back to the studio to join Tony on his show (just once more!), and heard him say yes to the idea of taking a handful of our people along with us. I was even more relieved to hear him insist that we would bring our own solicitor, Tom, along too. Somehow I felt that Tom just might help me keep a calming hand on Steve. As he said to Tony, by the time we came, Tom would have looked into just how, if at all, we could accept the financial help on offer, as this would only be considered on our terms.

And so, after a visit later in the day from my brother-in-law, Tom, a date was arranged for our trip to London. Tony had suggested that, as well as Tom, we should bring along a selection of our senior residents who felt up to answering viewers questions. He did ask if we would be bringing Will, but we felt best not as Lilly was getting closer by the day to her delivery date. As it seemed, she did still have a while to go, but both Ellen and myself had noticed the extra 'growth' she seemed to have put on recently, so suggested Will would be more use at the Grange, keeping things in order.

We planned on taking the mini-bus, so there was room to take Dave the plumber, Paul the counsellor, Josh our chef, and the pair of us. As it happened, Tom had some other business in London later that day, and so he chose to meet us there.

Knowing just how early we were having to leave, I had suggested that May shouldn't bother about getting up when we did, but she was determined to see us off. It was clear to both of us the tension in Steve over breakfast. We tried our best to distract him, but to no effect. Even Will coming up to crack jokes about his father having those make-up girls flapping around him, had no impact. Ok, he tried hard to put on a brave face, but I couldn't help thinking that he was reminiscent of a man going to the gallows, though I really couldn't decide if this was the worry about the Grange, or just the idea of facing the television cameras again!

I must own up to being somewhat relieved when it was time to leave, though still feeling concerned in case Steve made a run for it at the last minute, to find that Paul had insisted in doing the driving this time. As he said, he had been used to tackling the early morning traffic around London, and it would give the rest of us (really meaning Steve!) chance to get plenty of rest along the way. I don't know if it was a help or a hindrance that, hearing this, Will patted Steve on the back and remarked,

"There Dad, chance to catch up on your beauty sleep!"

Well, there we were, all made up, tidied up, and flapped over like a bunch of pop stars! Tony just found a brief minute to stick his head round the door to thank us, in particular Steve, and to wish us luck. I couldn't help thinking that, if we needed luck, that must mean he wasn't over optimistic, but I realised by the sneaky wink he gave me, that he really meant that he wished me luck in my quest to keep Steve under control this time! After all, the last time we'd appeared on his programme the poor man had all but been attacked! Even so, now that he'd got to spend time alone with him, I was sure he must realise that my Steve's bark is (usually) worse than his bite ... well, as long as I'm around to keep him under a little control! Little did he know that this had not always been the case.

He stopped just long enough to speak privately with Steve, Tom (who had actually arrived before us) and myself to explain that the businessman wanting to invest in our work would like a meeting in Tony's office when the programme was over.

Tom had been to Lansdown on regular visits, determined to keep a check of his 'big brother', and so had already met Paul, Dave and Josh. Being very much calmer and easy-going than his brother, Tom asked if we should talk tactics before going on stage in front of the cameras, but it came as no surprise to me to hear Steve's reply,

"Why? I'll just say what I bloody well think. That's tactics enough for me. What's wrong with straight talking after all?"

At this point I thought perhaps I should have a say about how we, including him, should behave if we hoped to gain support (financial or moral) from anyone.

"Now just you listen to me. The least you can do is listen to what they are offering. And then we can get Tom to decide what to do. Just you remember, and whatever is said on that stage, DO NOT lose it again! Do you hear me?"

Strangely enough, the smile he threw at me in exchange for that remark told everyone in our group that he meant, yes Mel; I saw a totally different meaning ... but that was private, to be 'discussed' in private between the two of us later; much later!

The next minute we were ushered onto the stage to be sat on a couple of sofas, with Steve and myself nearest Tony, and Tom and the others opposite. When the obligatory ad break finished, we were introduced by Tony. During the first minutes of his introduction he actually lowered his dignity by making a genuine and heartfelt apology to Steve for his previous attitude. As he explained, he had now been shown a side to the problems which Steve, myself and our staff do all we can to help less fortunate folk deal with.

"You no doubt remember the film we showed two weeks ago, following my time spent in the company of this remarkable man,"

I watched Steve carefully as he said this, quite expecting him to think, 'a lot of old flannel', and walk out, but I also caught a look pass from Tom to him which must have been by way of warning!

Tony went on to say that, now Steve was here, accompanied by his solicitor Mr Thomas Lockett, and Paul the counsellor, Dave the plumber, and Josh the chef, they have been kind enough to agree to answer a selection of viewers questions. Barely had he finished speaking when the lines were bombarded with calls from across the country!

Most were obviously directed at Steve, wanting to ask why he cared so much about these people. I must say how proud I was of the calm way he took and answered these, and with input from Tony, put over just why so many were in the position of being homeless. Tony was pleased to explain the facts as he'd learnt during his adventure.

When Paul was quizzed about his position at the Grange, he explained that he had served many years as an army counsellor, and therefore jumped at the chance to join Steve for the benefit of those in need of help. When asked about his presence at the Grange, Dave explained that, like a builder, carpenter, and market gardener, they had all met Steve when they were themselves homeless for different reasons, his being the firm going out of business, and having no home as he could no longer afford his rent.

Josh was proud to explain his relationship with Steve in full detail, right from that first day we met him, and how he was now fully qualified and head chef at the Grange. I felt such pride in him as I knew it was his case as much as any which had made Steve form the idea of finding a way to help such youngsters.

I have to admit to feeling relieved when after what seemed like an age, Tony rounded up the conversation, and the cameras finally faded away from us! We followed him off the stage and into a room where there was a good selection of sandwiches, tea or coffee, and comfortable chairs to relax in.

Chapter Forty-One

Following our rather early buffet lunch Tony came to fetch Steve, Tom and myself to meet our potential investor. As Tom said he was happy to bring us home after our meeting, Paul, Dave and Josh set off home in the mini-bus. It seemed that Josh had enjoyed a chat with the chef on set and taken careful note of quite a few ideas which he thought he might use the next time he had to cater for a party! I believed at that point all were content that we'd made a good impression on the viewers, but how much was yet to see. Before we went our separate ways, I was pleased to see Steve hand Paul a card along with instructions to stop before getting home to go in somewhere for a slap up meal (even if we really couldn't afford to be extravagant), for being so supportive.

Meanwhile the three of us were taken to meet a very smart looking fellow in an expensive looking suit. As soon as we entered the room he took a step toward Steve, arm outstretched, and introduced himself.

"Steven Lockett I presume? My name is Adam Saunders. And this must be Melanie?" he held his hand out to me.

"Mel, please. And this is my brother-in-law, Tom Lockett, our solicitor."

Adam Saunders shook Tom firmly by the hand, and said how good it was of us to come along and discuss his proposal. We all sat down around a table, listening to what he had to say. It seemed that Adam, as he insisted we call him, started his career from the very bottom, with no prospects at all. In fact, he had also spent the first year of his working life doing odd jobs for anyone who needed something done. During that time he had actually experienced the problems of living rough, until finding an opportunity to earn by doing deliveries for cash-in-hand jobs! As he admitted, some of these were quite possibly not even legal, but allowed him chance to earn enough to rent a room somewhere. From there he had worked up a business, originally doing deliveries, then moving into sales, and now was managing director of a multi-national company.

"So you see Steve, I'm not going into this plan with my eyes closed. Like you, I feel that more people should be given the chance to pick themselves up and re-build their lives, and if we can find a way I can help you do this I will be more than happy to do so."

I could see Steve was at the very least, considering what the man had said, and I suppose that was progress of some sort. Even so, I also could see that it would take a lot of persuasion to ease just a tiny bit of control from him! I really couldn't say I blamed him; after all, we'd worked hard over many years to build the Grange to what it was now, but in doing so we had put nearly every spare penny we had into it. It had almost got to the stage now where we were having to rely on our ongoing income as silent partners with Jake's brother, Andy, in his business, which until this time we had kept as our personal 'pocket money' as it were, leaving all other funds purely for the running of the Grange.

Adam went on to explain the struggle he'd had to convince people to invest in his business from the start, even to take him seriously, but he'd been like Steve (downright stubborn!), and ignored their prejudice and carried on regardless, eventually finding the break he needed when just one person saw his potential sufficiently enough to make a small investment which was all it took to help him climb the ladder of success.

I could see Steve was about to start bringing up his arguments against the idea of letting anyone into what he knew was purely his, or should I say, our, business. I felt that if he didn't use a little of the one quality he lacked ... tact, this could all go wrong. As it happened I wasn't the only one with the same thought, Tom was quick off the mark and jumped in.

"Though I am Steve's brother Mr Saunders, I am also his solicitor. I believe I am right in explaining that, though Lansdown Grange quite obviously is in need of some investment, having been completely restored and converted to the use and standard my brother and his wife have managed to do over the years since he inherited it, he now finds himself in a difficult position. Even so, or perhaps because of this, he remains adamant that there is absolutely no way he is prepared to release control of ownership or the work carried out there."

I could see that Adam Saunders was impressed to hear just how well Tom managed to put our case over, whilst at the same time I felt he clearly saw the stubborn, yet anxious look on Steve's face as he did this. I believe I detected a flash of understanding cross his face as he looked across at Steve to say,

"Yes Steve; I do know exactly where you're coming from. I too had a couple of times over the years when investors wanted to take over my business, but after working so hard to build it up there was no way that was going to happen! No, what I had in mind was that, with your brother here in charge of setting it up and heading it, we could find a group of people to act as trustees to oversee a charitable trust, which you could call on as needed to support your work."

At this point Tony jumped in to say that, if this was done, he had already had others who would be keen to invest. When Steve queried them as to why Adam, or anyone else would want to do this, Adam explained that there were certain benefits to him. He would be able to claim tax benefits, and it wouldn't do his reputation any harm either! As he added, he would have no objection to perhaps taking the odd youngster under his wing if they showed any interest in joining one of his companies. As he said, there are always openings for those keen to learn.He was quick to assure us that he had absolutely no interest in interfering with our work, though he would love to visit at some point to see it for himself.

By the time we'd sat for the best part of the afternoon with Tony and Adam, with much needed guidance from Tom, we eventually left with heads spinning! On the way back to where Tom had left his car, we stopped for a good, slap-up meal to help us recover from the long, mentally exhausting day, before setting off home.

It was not until we were back in the car and on our way home that I remembered that I'd put my mobile on silent this morning, not wanting it to ring during the programme. I fished it from my pocket and pressed the side button. To my horror I found I'd missed six calls from Will, but then there was a text just saying 'ring me'!

I knew Lilly had been suffering odd pains the previous day, as Ellen told her, the body's way to warn you of upcoming labour! Oh goodness, I hope she's ok. I told Steve and Tom and then rang Will immediately!

"Are you ok, is Lilly alright Will; I'm sorry, I left this switched off all day and forgot to put it back on. Is it the baby?"

An unmistakably happy voice greeted me on the end,

"Yes Mum, we're more than fine; and so is our son! He's here already ... nearly a week early too! He's amazing Mum, you wait till you see him. He arrived at eight-forty this morning. Bob and Ellen took us to the hospital. I wish you could have been there ... it was amazing Mum!"

I couldn't help laughing at his jubilation, and I'd put my phone on speaker so Steve and Tom could hear about it too. Typical of Steve, he couldn't resist saying,

"And you're telling me you didn't pass out watching it then son?"

"Huh! No of course I didn't. Mind you, I did feel a little bit squeamish, but Lilly squeezed my hand so tight it kept me focussed!"

We congratulated them both and said we would see them in the morning. This news had the effect of lightening an otherwise confused, rather stressful day. We were now grandparents!!

Chapter Forty-Two

We arrived home that night almost at the same time as our fellow grandparents, Ellen and Bob. They had both been at the hospital since taking Lilly and Will that morning. I admit to feeling a little envious of them being there just when we were away, but then after all they were parents of the new mother, and we knew that by the next morning we would all be one big family, brought together by this tiny mite who Will had sent us a string of photos of on my phone! It seemed that Will had sent some to May on the phone we'd recently bought her, and then rang to talk her through how to open them! I don't think I'd seen her so excited since the day her errant son, Steve, turned up on her doorstep after a two year absence!

It seemed that the news of the baby had spread long before we arrived as we were met by quite a crowd, cheering as if we were responsible for her arrival. It was a really great homecoming, and one, I for one hoped, would be a sign of new beginnings for us all. Tom came upstairs with us before heading home to have a (in his case very small) drink to celebrate the baby. After all, as he said, it wouldn't do for a solicitor to be caught drink driving.

At one point May turned to Steve and asked how we had got on. I wish I could have heard him say that everything was fine, but this was Steve ... and you must know my Steve by now; hard to convince about anything that wasn't his own idea! All she got by way of a response was,

"I'm thinking about it."

I overheard Tom tell her quietly before he left that it all sounded good, and that he was positive he could get everything done in a secure fashion which would be in everyone's best interest and keep Steve in charge of Lansdown and his work. As long as his brother agreed, he would get it sorted.

That night, as the baby came so much earlier than expected, Lilly had been kept in for observation. Will chose to stay with his new family. Consequently we said that we would go there the next morning to bring them home. I could hardly wait to see what the newest member of the Lockett family was like. Photos are one thing, but nothing compared to the feeling of seeing that tiny, warm little bundle, wrapped up cosily in the cot next to Lilly, and knowing he was our grandson.

"Go on Mel," Lilly told me, obviously knowing how badly I wanted to, "Pick him up and say hello."

I certainly didn't need telling twice. He had his eyes closed in the cot, but as soon as I lifted him gently into my arms, he opened them, and there they were ... those same piercing brown ones both his father and grandfather had! I must admit to being a little shocked as I'd always been given to believe that babies were always born with blue ones, but then Will wasn't I remember.

"Do you know what you're going to call him yet," I asked.

"Well, we did have an idea, but ..."

"But what?"

"Well, Lilly had wondered about Robert, after her Dad."

I said what a good idea, but could see he had something else on his mind. When I pushed him a bit more it seemed they didn't want to make Steve feel left out!

"Don't be silly. I won't be offended. In fact I have a suggestion for a second name, if you want one that is?"

They looked from one another, then at Steve.

"How about Peter, after your grandfather. Only a thought mind you. It's for you to decide."

"Dad, we had sort of wondered about that, but didn't want to make you feel left out.

In the end, I think as much for May's sake as Steve's, Peter Robert Lockett. I don't think I've ever seen May happier than when she first set eyes on her new Great-grandson, Peter Robert, later that morning.

By the following morning, once things settled down from all the excitement over the new arrival, we sat chatting to May over breakfast. She remarked just how good it felt now to have another member of the family, and how it made the whole place feel even more like home. It seemed that this jogged her memory about our trip to London.

"So now Steve, you still haven't told me how things went with that chap you spoke to about the help he was offering?"

Trying to brush this aside, he said,

"Well, he was ok I suppose. Better than I expected; but …"

"But what? What did Tom think?

Obviously not really keen to talk about it if he could avoid it, he had to tell her,

"Well, he seemed to think it might be ok if I let him work on it to get it right, but …"

Clearly getting a little exasperated, she turned to him saying,

"Will you stop saying 'but'! Stop being so negative."

Steve gave her a quizzical look over his coffee cup as she said that, and so she answered his questioning look by asking him,

"Think; what colour are negatives? Black. What did your father call you? ... His rainbow boy; and where did he tell you a rainbow leads?"

Steve looked like the little boy he must have been when his father called him that as he answered,

"To your hopes and dreams, but ..."

May heaved a sigh, then went on,

"Never mind 'but'. Tell me Steve, just what are your hopes and dreams?"

"Well Mum, I thought that was pretty obvious, just to keep Lansdown Grange going."

May patted the big, strong hand near hers on the table, then said simply,

"Then its simple dear, it seems you wanted your fathers advice last week, perhaps this is his way of giving it. You know what he'd say now? Stop being so stubborn, accept the help on offer, and let your hopes and dreams lead you to the end of your rainbow! After all, what harm can it do my dear?"

I could see that her words were truly making him think. At least, he stopped saying 'but', and went out that morning promising to ring Tom as soon as he came in later. While he was gone I just couldn't resist popping down to visit our new grandson. Little Peter Robert was truly gorgeous and, although they say that what seems like a smile, at that age is probably wind, I'll swear that as I looked down at him in my arms, he did actually wink at me! Yes, no doubt about it ... he was definitely another Lockett! One thing was certain, that living at Lansdown he would never be short of admirers or people queueing up to babysit him if the need arose.

Clearly, Ellen and Bob were as excited at becoming grandparents as we were, and in some strange way, this tiny person seemed to have the effect of bringing the whole population of Lansdown into an even tighter feeling of community. Now all that was needed was to persuade Steve to take a chance on allowing Tom to go ahead with Adam Saunders to set up a charitable trust; purely on the understanding that full ownership and control of our work stayed in Steve's hands of course!

With this (and May's words) in mind, later that morning, Tom popped over with some paperwork for Steve to sign, just in preparation as he assured his brother! On Steve's suggestion, I believe feeling that being a father now put him 'almost' on a level pegging with him, he insisted that Will should now officially be made our business manager. As he pointed out, Will was well qualified to keep the accounts and other paperwork up to date. He would then be able to liaise with Tom between us and Adam's finance people. Secretly I did wonder just how much he'd do without some interference from his father, but if anyone could cope with that it would be Will.

Of course, when Tom came he brought his wife Margaret to be introduced to the newest Lockett. To save May the exertion of going down to Lilly and Will's bungalow, Lilly brought the baby up to our rooms to meet his wider family, and I split my time between chatting to them and popping in and out of the office (just to check that Steve was behaving himself!). By the end of the afternoon I was relieved to find that Tom had managed to act as go-between and come to an arrangement which suited both parties. We could now give a huge sigh of relief and get on with the work we loved so much.

Lansdown Grange was safe at last!

The next day was a Sunday and, other than his early exercise session (weekends made no difference to my Steve!), I had an idea to help him unwind from the last few weeks stress. Lilly and Will had asked May to go to theirs for the day, to spend time with little Peter Robert, so we would be on our own. The sun was shining, and it was turning out to be the warmest day we'd had so far that spring.

"Tell you what Steve, I've got an idea."

He looked up from the paperwork he was idly flicking through on his desk,

"What sort of idea is that? Go back to bed?"

"No, of course not! Don't you ever think of anything else?"

He crossed the room and put his arm round me,

"No; why, should I when I've got you to myself all day?"

It was good to see the old twinkle back in his eyes after the last few weeks.

"What I reckon is that we should pack a picnic and go out for a good walk.

So that's what we did. Not wanting to bother driving, we decided to put a rug and picnic in our two rucksacks, and make a complete hike all the way round the lake, starting where I'd fallen from the broken bridge. It had been rebuilt a few months after I'd nearly drowned following its collapse, so it seemed appropriate to try the new one!

For once I managed to slow him to nearer my pace than his army route march one! It was a lovely, relaxing feeling just strolling along between the trees, stopping half way just to sit and listen to the birds in the trees above us. The feeling of being just the two of us, away from all the hustle and bustle we'd been surrounded with of late, had exactly the effect I'd hoped for. After all the years of hard work, as much as we loved it so much, I don't think either of us realised just how long it had been since we'd actually had quality time alone, so we made this time count and promised one another to do it more often.

By the time we'd completed our slow trek around the perimeter of the lake, coming back to the point from which we'd began, we spread the rug on that same mossy bank where Steve had made love to me for the very first time. This time we ate our picnic and sat together with his arm round me. Just as I knew he would, he turned up my face to his and kissed me in the same tender way he had that first time.

I knew just what to expect next of course … but then, I looked over his shoulder.

"Hey look Steve."

He turned and looked where I was pointing. There, clearly coming through the clouds was a rainbow!

"See where the rainbow ends Steve? It's going down behind the trees … pointing at Lansdown Grange!"

I truly believe that the love I felt from him that day was stronger, deeper and yet more tender than I'd ever known before.

Printed in Great Britain
by Amazon